A Texas Beach Town Romance

Written by
USA Today bestselling author
Daryl Banner

Far From Paradise

A Texas Beach Town Romance

Cover Photographer

Eric Battershell Photography

Cover Model

Drew Truckle

Cover & Interior Design

Daryl Banner

FAR FROM PARADISE
CHAPTERS

FOREWORD

First off, thank you so much for picking up this book, and I can't wait for you to spend a fun and steamy weekend down here in this balmy Texas beach town!

Now it's time to set aside your stresses, forget your job or responsibilities or worries, pack a figurative bag, and come on down to Dreamwood Isle, the Texas beach town where you're about to go on vacation for the next twenty chapters. Enjoy your stay, don't forget your sunscreen, and happy reading, always!

XXOO
Daryl

AUTHOR & COMPOSER
ROMANCE / FANTASY / DYSTOPIAN

Far from
PARADISE

CHAPTER 1

SEANY

THE CITY OF SAN ANTONIO SPINS AWAY IN THE WINDOW.

And with it, memories of sleepless nights.

Sweat in my eyes.

Garbage bins.

Shopping carts that contain someone's entire life.

The stench of wasteful tourists and rancid beer floating in the air like smoke.

Large cardboard boxes that once housed a shipment of deli napkins, now housing a whole human being, becoming a home with no real address.

Under a bridge where paranoid men sleep with stolen restaurant steak knives held by their sides.

I watch it all go away through the window of the bus.

Clenching a backpack to my chest—my own figurative shopping cart, containing everything I own in this world.

Everything I have left.

Plus the bus ticket pinched between my dirty fingers, the first legitimate thing I've bought in weeks, the thing I saved up actual money for, my ticket to somewhere else.

Somewhere better.

Somewhere far from here.

No one is seated next to me, nor behind me. I feel like a real human being again, even if it's temporary, sitting on this air-conditioned bus among other human beings.

But it may not be a coincidence I'm sitting alone.

I probably smell like everything I hate.

And look worse.

It's funny, how people will turn their nose up at you, even if it's obvious you're suffering, or down on your luck, or just in a bad place. As if poverty is a disease. As if a set of terrible circumstances is a virus you can catch.

I notice a woman across the aisle. She keeps sneaking glances at me—an older woman with curly white hair, like cotton balls, with papery, pale skin and tiny glasses. A total grandma. Next to her, an old man staring out the window, probably her husband, a total grandpa.

The woman smiles at me, her eyes twinkling.

I look away.

And squeeze my backpack tighter.

It's a while later that the bus pulls into a small rest area off the highway. "Fifteen minutes and we're back on the road, folks," calls out the bus driver, hoarse and tired.

After a trip to the men's room, I stop by an old vending machine next to a bench and stare at the ridiculous price of a fucking single Milky Way bar. Even a bottle of water is stupid expensive.

I peer down at the two crinkled dollars and couple of mismatched coins on my palm.

I can endure the hunger a little longer. Maybe I'll score something when I get to my next place.

Wherever that is.

The elderly lady from the bus is sitting on the bench, waiting on her old fart of a husband. Her sweet, nice eyes are on me again. Two bottles of water sit next to her on the bench, beads of condensation running down their sides.

My throat puckers.

She lifts her eyebrows and faces me fully. "Sonny, you want one of these bottles? I really don't like to drink too much. It'll make me have to pee and Lord knows I can't dream of using that cramped bus bathroom."

My eyes are on that bottle like a starving dog to a bone.

"No, thanks," I mumble before stuffing my cash away into a pocket and trudging back to the bus.

Another hour on the road, and I'm regretting my utter inability to trust anyone's kindness. What am I so worried about? She offered me a free bottle of water. I should have taken it. I should take anything that's given freely to me. It is literally how guys in situations like mine get by.

Something in me is hardening, though.

Like I need to prove something to myself. I gotta resist any instinct of mine that wants others' help. I can't rely on anyone or anything. Even this old lady is just in my life for a fleeting moment of time—one end of this bus ride to the other, then gone.

I shut my eyes and hug my backpack even tighter. The tighter I hug it, the less I can feel the growl in my stomach.

Instead of a growl, I hear a snore.

I peer to my side to find the old woman across the aisle again. Her husband is dead asleep, head leaning against the window, and he's running wood through a table saw with every labored snore. The old woman, sweet as can be, only hums to herself as she gently rummages through a small bag in her lap. She has endured much of his snoring, every night, every naptime, every lazy afternoon. I can tell.

She spots me looking at her, but doesn't make much of a deal out of it, continuing to hum as she searches through her bag. She pulls out a wrapped sandwich, then considers it for a while. She lets out an oddly long and demonstrative sigh, then eyes me. "You hungry, sonny?"

My usual quick wit is dried up on my tongue. In a tiny moment of weakness, I only stare back at her, silent.

"My husband always complains about my sandwiches. Not enough this. Too much that. I swear, a Michelin star deli couldn't satisfy his taste. Do you want this?"

I swallow hard. "No, I'm—"

She extends the thick and delicately wrapped sandwich across the aisle. "Go ahead, sonny. Do me a favor and take this off my hands, will you?"

Before I can answer, she simply lays the sandwich on my lap, then returns to fishing through her bag. A moment later, she produces one of the water bottles she had from the rest area and sets it on my seat next to me. It's balanced precariously, and only a couple seconds after she lets go, it starts to tip. I grab it, stopping it from falling. After closing up her bag, she looks off toward the window in silence.

I lick my lips, overcome. Then I unwrap the sandwich as slowly as I can force myself to—fighting my urge to tear off the plastic covering like a rabid wolf—and bring it to my mouth for a bite.

A sweet, tasty, perfect bite.

The lettuce crunches with life.

The tomatoes snap with fresh succulence.

The bread, as soft and chewy as fresh-made.

I barely chew the first bite, swallowing it too fast. I pop open the bottle of water quickly and chug a quarter of it down. Then I'm right back on the sandwich, delirious with gratitude as I relish mouthful after mouthful.

That's when I catch the old woman looking at me.

She smiles delightfully. "You remind me of one of my grandsons. I think it's the dimples."

I swallow my bite. "Your husband's fucking nuts if he doesn't like your sandwich." My eyes go big. "S-Sorry for cursing like that."

"Ain't anything I haven't heard before." She nods. "I was serious about that water. I can't risk a single sip. But my husband always insist we have water on us at all times. Don't mind me," she says quickly. "Eat, eat, eat. Don't let my mindless prattling interrupt your lunch."

I take a bite, this time less vigorously, more in control of myself. "Thanks," I mumble through my mouthful.

"Where are you headed to, sonny? Can I ask?"

I stop chewing.

Can I ask …?

The way she worded that tells me everything. She must know I'm homeless or on the run. She can probably smell it all over me—that I'm in a situation, that I'm in need. The sandwich I'm eating and the water bottle I'm chugging are charity. She wants the mystery solved. She wants me to tell her the rest of the story she'll probably share at whatever family gathering she's headed to. *'Oh, it was so sad, I gave my sandwich to this poor, lonely boy on the bus …'*

"On the other hand," she goes on, "you don't have to tell me anything. I *did* just say I didn't want to interrupt your lunch. You know what?" She lifts a hand. "I'm gonna sit here and just enjoy the roar of the bus engine while you eat." She smiles, quite satisfied with herself. Her husband's snoring reaches a new and impressive depth, causing her eyes to turn funny. "Well, the roar of *something*, for sure."

This may come as a surprise, but I like making people feel good.

Even bad people, sometimes.

Like my dad.

So I decide to give the woman what she wants to hear. "I'm on the way to my Uncle Don's house," I tell her. She perks right up at my words, facing me again. "He lives in a nice house … a nice house near the beach with two dogs, King and Rook. Didn't want to spend too much money on the road, since I'm short on cash. So … I really appreciate the sandwich and water." I take another bite, smile through it, and nod. "Thank you."

The woman studies me for a while, eyes twinkling with wonder. "Your uncle sounds nice," she decides to say.

"Yeah, my Uncle Don is pretty cool." I try to imagine a perfect uncle. "He likes baking. He bakes a pan of cookies every Sunday morning. Mmm, I can't *wait* to taste them again. They're just classic chocolate chip, but I swear he puts something else in them. Mmm, they're the best. Must be love … his secret ingredient." I chuckle, imagining this memory that doesn't exist, yet touches me as if it does.

"Ever since Aunt Amy passed away, he likes when I visit and help him around the house. I'll clean out his gutters for him, rake the lawn, and walk both the dogs. King's getting big. Rook is a little thing. I'm ..." I go for another bite and chew it quickly as my imagination runs wild. I have had many nights to dream of a lovely life. "I'm coming back from a ... a church trip to San Antonio. You can say I like giving back to my community. My uncle says I've got a big heart, but ... I don't think I'm all that special. It's important we all try to put some good out into the world. It's what the world needs most." I take another swig of water, then another big bite.

"Well, well. That sounds lovely, sonny."

Her nickname for me is starting to catch on. Sounds like "sunny". I've always liked sunshine. It's my favorite thing to see every morning on the streets.

It indicates an end to another terrible, restless night.

"You know, sonny ... life is full of choices," she says. "Good ones. Bad ones. Difficult and easy ones. It's all part of the journey of growing up. I think it's a mighty fine goal of yours, to *choose* to put good out into the world, just like you say ... no matter what it is you do."

My chewing slows.

"I know you may think I'm just some old lady on a bus who has more yesterdays than tomorrows, but I see hope in your eyes, and ... and I see brightness in your future."

8

Hope in my eyes. Brightness in my future.

I wonder suddenly if she's smarter than I took her for and didn't believe a word of my lie.

"You will face many more struggles in life," she goes on. "Some will be the simple choice of whether to accept a sandwich from an old lady on a bus. Other struggles will seem insurmountable. Perhaps you've faced a few already. But please, allow an old lady *her* chance to put some good out into the world before her time's up."

She reaches across the aisle and touches my arm.

I flinch and stare at her, wide-eyed.

"Do you need a place to stay tonight, sonny?" she asks so softly, the engine of the bus nearly steals her words.

I clutch her flavorsome achievement of bread, lettuce, and lunchmeat in my dirty hands. Her fingers are cold, yet her eyes are blazing warm. I smell her homemade cookies. I feel her tucking me into a safe, soft bed. I hear the hum of a TV in the other room where she and her husband sleep. I experience all of that, just with a peek into her eyes.

This is one of those struggles. One of those *choices*.

To those warm, blazing eyes, I give her my answer: "I-I'm going to my Uncle Don's. H-He's expecting me."

She doesn't move for a while, still staring at me. As if waiting. Giving me one last chance before the door closes.

Then she gives me a crushed, sweet, saccharine smile I will remember for weeks to come. "Of course, sonny."

It's the last exchange we have.

After I finish the sandwich, I pack away what remains of the water for later. For the rest of the way, we ride in silence, enjoying the roar of the engine—and her husband's snores, which have since grown softer, as if the man has finally found a pleasant dream.

I hope I find mine, too.

Soon, the destination is reached, and everyone gets off the bus. I don't wait for the old woman, hurrying off in the first direction I find. I pass intersections, gas stations, and strip malls. Where do I go now? As I stroll aimlessly along the road, I consider the cash in my pocket, the backpack over my shoulder, and how many minutes I have left of the sun sitting up there in the sky.

How long will I wander before I find where I belong?

How many more bus rides? How many more nice old ladies? How many more sleepless nights?

I stop at the last intersection before a causeway, where the sight of the Gulf of Mexico takes me by surprise. I gaze at it in wonder, a hopeless dream swelling in my heart. The salty air tosses my bangs and makes me aware of the dirt on my skin. I think of how good it might feel to have those cool waves racing over my bare feet, cleansing my weary body ... Will it ever be possible to feel happy again?

A hanging sign by the road creaks as the wind blows, as if in answer. *Dreamwood Isle*, it reads.

CHAPTER 2

COOPER

SOMETHING'S MISSING.

My nuts, to be precise.

That's three cans of salted nuts to go with a twelve-pack of Pepsi that went missing yesterday. Do I have a thief on my hands now? I'll be damned if it's any of my small, trusted handful of employees here at the bar, but you never know. We've all fallen on hard times.

"Boss, the front's getting busy."

I sigh at my shelves, then turn to face Mars—short for Marcia. Her pixie-like face is hugged by a curly, frazzled mane of dark brown hair, her tawny skin sleek with sweat.

She's a godsend. I'm thankful her taqueria-running mom can send her over to help me on busy nights like these.

"Something wrong?" she asks.

I swipe a can of nuts off the shelf. "Just missing some inventory. Not sure how."

"Hmm. Haven't seen anyone back here all afternoon other than you, me, and Chase." She makes a face. "Well, there *is* some shady underage dude who's sneaking around the bar for the past few hours. Had to kick him out twice already."

I lift an eyebrow. "Shady underage dude …?"

"My age, eighteen if I had to guess, definitely not old enough to drink. Cute as a button, but I don't trust him."

Just as I'm about to point out that it's the weekend and teenagers are gonna find their way in one way or another, my lead bartender Chase pops in with his tanned, freckled cheeks and messy, sandy-blond bangs. "Uh … guys? It's, like, hella busy out here and the—"

"I already told him," says Mars.

"Oh." Chase blinks his pretty, dopey eyes at me. It's a wonder he's so good with making drinks and counting money, because he doesn't seem to have much else going on upstairs. But I like him because he's great for business; his face brings in the customers.

"It's all good," I assure them. "I'm done here. Chase, refill the bowls." I slap the can of nuts into his hand. "If this is any indication of what we're in for, it'll be ten times worse when evening rolls in."

An hour later, I hate that I'm right.

I'm behind the counter taking order after order with no rest. Something special must be going on this weekend in Dreamwood Isle. This quaint and balmy Texas beach town always gets a fresh wave of visitors every weekend, but it's been quite a while since I've seen it get *this* busy. The Easy Breezy is built to take a good number of thirsty clientele off of Breezeway Point, the main tourist beach on the south end of the island, but I'm pretty sure I'll be breaking a fire code or two by the time the sun sets.

No matter how busy it gets, I'm never stressed. That's the whole vibe I maintain here at the Easy Breezy: just smile, kick back with your friends, and enjoy a good time with a nice, cold drink in your hand. The beach is visible through the wraparound windows, some of which are left open to take in the salty air, the distant noise of crashing waves, and the endless sight of people walking along the sand or nearby boardwalk. What more could you ask for?

A familiar face cuts through the crowd. It's Adrian, a friend who used to work here as my lead bartender before Chase. Square-jawed and confident, he's built like a lost demigod son of Poseidon with blue diamonds for eyes. His dress shirt and tie suggest he's on his break from his job at Thalassa, an upscale seafood restaurant on the boardwalk.

He comes to the front and folds his big arms on the bar, muscles bulging in his sleeves. "Busy here too, huh?"

I slide a drink to a customer. "Pride weekend."

"Need a hand?"

"Aren't you on break?"

"Fuck it, I'm giving you a hand." He hops around the counter and gets right to work. I smirk and shake my head, then tend to a group of guys asking for another round. Of course I won't turn down help when it's needed. Besides, Adrian knows what he's doing.

My eyes are caught by a face in the back of the room— a face that instantly doesn't seem to belong. You can call it my observant nature, but I know partiers when I see them. I know horny guys looking for a hookup. I know awkward guys and I know deep-pocketed vacationers.

This face is none of those things.

Sweet eyes, yet guarded. Messy light brown hair, fair yet sun-kissed complexion, and clothes one size too big for his petite frame. Hands stuffed in his pockets, he scopes the room like a hawk, keen and watchful. His stillness makes him stick out among the constant movement and madness.

Then he slips away—and I lose him. Where'd he go? Was that the shady kid Mars mentioned?

"I don't know how you're still single," says Adrian as he finishes up with another customer. "You must have fifty numbers passed to you on bar napkins every weekend."

More like a hundred, but who's counting? "Adrian ... Taking advantage of young drunk men isn't my thing," I remind him as I slide a glass under the tap. "Maybe back in my twenties I would've entertained a few options, but I'm far from twenty and reminded more of that fact each day."

"Far from twenty? C'mon. You're barely thirty."

"Try pushing forty."

"Oh." Adrian snorts. "You really *are* a grandpa, huh?"

I jab him in the ribs for that. "Make another old man joke and I'll put you over my knee and spank you 'til you learn your lesson."

"Promise?"

The truth is, there's been a gaping hole in my life for quite some time. I tend to assume it's filled with my baby: the Easy Breezy bar. But when I go home, I feel as empty as the bottles and glasses I clean up before shutting this place down for the night. The line of potted plants on my back porch—each of which are named and dutifully cared for every day—are likely another consequence of having no one in my life to call my own. I give them all my love.

I hate to admit that Adrian might have a point.

Maybe I need something to care for that doesn't come confined in a clay pot.

But tonight, my focus is elsewhere. My eyes skip over the crowd for that kid again with no luck. Why does it matter anyway? He can't possibly be the thief. How would he get into my inventory, anyway? Maybe he's just another bored teen separated from his pals, likely staying at one of the cheaper hotels at the north end of the island. It's the last week of June, and there are tons of Pride events all over the island—as well as the boys that come with them.

"You coming to the bonfire thing after the weekend?"

Adrian's question pulls me out of my thoughts. "Nah."

"Don't know why I asked. You never come anyway."

"I see my fair share of people every day. No need to stand around a fire on the beach drinking beer until three in the morning bitching about the latest wave of vacationers."

He snorts at that. "You need some rest and relaxation, my man. Running this bar seven days a week doesn't do you good. I don't care how old you are, no one deserves to be alone forever. Hey, just a few hours ago, I served this lovely couple of men in their fifties. They fed each other bites of buttery lobster. How fuckin' adorable is that?"

Hmm. Adorable ...

I glance at the window, the boardwalk visible in the far distance across the sand, with all its glittering lights against the waning early evening sunlight. I always had this vision of walking along that boardwalk hand-in-hand with a man I love—whoever that is. Every time I imagine it, I feel just a little happier.

And every time I imagine it, I feel a little emptier.

I'll be damned if I ever admit that out loud.

16

"Hey, Adrian, have you seen a teen around here?" I ask between customers, shifting gears back to a more pressing matter at hand. "Eighteen. Smallish guy. Sweet-faced …"

He quirks an eyebrow. "You're not really narrowing it down much. That's half this weekend's twink population."

"He looks like he doesn't belong here. Out of place."

"No one belongs here."

I'm letting my imagination go wild. I probably just miscounted my items or typed something into the computer wrong. It's all in my head. "Never mind."

"Crap. Lost track of the time, break's almost up." He slaps a hand on my back. "You got this, right?"

Just then, I spot the kid again on the other side of the room. He's got a drink in his hand, and he—

Wait a second. That's not a drink. That's a can of nuts.

My nuts.

As if sensing me, the kid looks my way.

Our eyes lock.

His reflect curiosity.

Then fear.

Then outright defiance.

Before I can flinch, he takes off out the door, flinging it open so hard, it smacks against the wall with a noise that draws startled looks.

I'm not letting him get away.

Not this time.

"Watch the bar," I say quickly before rushing around the counter and tearing after the kid. I'm pretty sure Adrian lets out a protest, but I don't hear a word of it.

I fly through the doors and onto the porch. With a glance either way, I don't see any sign of him. I make a snap decision and head toward the beach, figuring if I was a thief, I'd be headed into unlit, crowded areas to hide. My eyes scan the cuddled couples and clusters of men scattered all over the shore, laughing, drinking, and hanging around in the fiery orange sunset that sets the beach ablaze.

Couples everywhere.

Lovebirds everywhere.

Happy men holding hands. Happy men kissing. Happy men with arms around each other's backs. Throuples, too.

Yet no sign of the thief.

I could easily just let this go. It's just one can of nuts, right? Maybe a few sodas this past week. I shouldn't make a big thing out of it.

But I apparently can't help myself tonight. Something has come over me. Aren't I generous enough to the people of this island without having to have my nuts stolen out from under my damned nose? There's nothing I hate worse than being taken advantage of.

Those are *my* nuts that little thief has in his hands.

CHAPTER 3

SEANY

I PRESS MY BACK FLAT TO THE WALL AND WAIT.

My stomach growls.

I wrench open the can, scoop out some salted peanuts, and pop them into my mouth. Rejuvenation pours into my body like sweet love, all the way down to my bones, as I chew and taste the flavorful, seasoned goodness on my tongue. I slowly slide down to the ground as I hug the can, then scoop another generous helping into my mouth.

I've been watching him for days. I've seen how he is with people. Caring. Compassionate. Giving. I was almost certain he wouldn't care about one measly can of peanuts going missing—until I caught his eyes across the room and realized he wasn't having it.

His name is Cooper, but locals call him Coop. He also lives somewhere on the island, and from what I've heard, he's a single gay man. I can't imagine what effect being single has on a gay man in a beach town full of beautiful men—yet he never seems to pursue anyone, even guys who throw themselves at him across the bar. I notice. Is he grieving a lost lover from his past? Has he sworn off men?

Cooper is a total mystery to me. All I know is, he's a good person. And I've just stolen from him for the second time. Or is it the third ...?

"It'll be the last time," I tell myself through a mouthful of peanuts, chewing vigorously. "I won't steal again. I will figure out a way to survive that doesn't hurt anyone."

But how can I hope to do that? No one's door is open, figuratively or otherwise. If anything living on the streets of San Antonio for the past three months has taught me, it's that no one's compassion comes free.

I find myself thinking yet again of that old woman on the bus. Maybe I made the wrong choice that day. I should have admitted I had nowhere to sleep. I should've accepted her help—but instead, I was my usual stubborn, wary self.

It's hard to believe that was a whole month ago.

I've learned that sometimes when the world won't give you what you need to survive, you have to take it.

The law sees that as stealing.

I see it as making it to the next day.

Still: "It'll be the last time," I repeat, a touch firmer. "I won't steal again. I will figure out a way to—"

The sound of footsteps jabbing into sand stirs my ears.

I twist my head. Cooper has spotted me.

Every thought flees my head as I tear away from the wall and run. "Hey!" he shouts. Does he seriously expect me to stop and answer him? I dart across the sand, feeling him on my heels with every step. I reach a line of cabanas facing the beach and weave through them. "Hey! Stop!"

Sorry, Coop, but there's no way I'm stopping.

I hear him stumble and fall with a grunt, which only makes me pause for a second to look over my shoulder. I give him one wince of an apology before I keep running. As I round the corner of an outdoor shower and bathroom, I realize I'll run a lot faster without holding this can, so I start scooping handful after handful of salted peanuts past my lips as I run, then finally toss the can over my shoulder and pick up speed. I don't even get to enjoy them as I chew with urgency and run, run, run.

It's quite a while before I lose him. I might be on the opposite side of the whole damned island by now. Coop's got a lot of stamina for an older guy.

I'm almost sorry I put him through that.

I plop down on the sand, right in the middle of a bunch

of people who are soaking in every last second of the sun as it sets beyond the watery horizon. I hug my knees to my chest and scowl, still hungry. Maybe I could have run even with the can of nuts, but I just panicked and tossed them. I regret it now. A few handfuls didn't curb the hunger.

Truth is, I'm not ready to get in serious trouble at yet one more location I've found. I need this place to work. It's got everything I need: constantly shifting crowds, wasteful hotels with dumpsters full of treasure, parks, beaches …

Loads of hot men walking around. Tons of wandering eyes. *And plenty of left-behind belongings …*

"Hey there."

I glance to my right. It's some cute guy around my age sitting on a blanket next to me, a book in his lap. He lowers his shades—which he doesn't need at all, considering only a modest sliver of orange, glowing sunlight remains.

"How's it going?" he asks.

Is he trying to pick me up? I can never tell if I'm being flirted with. "Fine. Just enjoying the waves, I guess."

"Tell me about it. This place is like paradise, huh? My boyfriend and I have only been here for a short time, but it feels like we've been here forever."

I nod slowly, not really looking at him. But I do notice he's alone. "Where's your boyfriend?"

"Took a trip to the bathroom. Too many piña coladas," he adds with a chuckle.

I guess that's supposed to be a joke. "Cool."

I feel his elbow nudge my side. "Hey, you alright? You look kinda down. No one in all of Dreamwood Isle should ever be down."

The best part about talking to strangers is getting to say anything and throw away your emotions. It's free therapy. "This place is what everyone in San Antonio said it'd be."

"Is that where you're from?"

Nope. "Yep."

"I'm from a little town called Spruce. You've probably never heard of it. So what did everyone in San Antonio say this place is like?"

I eye the blanket he's lying on. It's a Pac-Man blanket.

Also, all of that about San Antonio was bullshit. Didn't even know this place existed until I found it. "Paradise."

"Hey, that's what I just said it's like!" He lets out a laugh, then draws quiet, studying me. "So what's wrong?"

"I'm here at last, sitting in the middle of it all, and I feel ..." I hug my knees tighter. "... *so* far from paradise."

"Oh. Maybe you just need to give it time. You lonely? Who'd you come here with? I'm Toby, by the way."

I already forgot his name. "I'm here with no one."

"Hmm. You wanna hang with me and my boyfriend?" He takes off his shades and sets them on top of a balled-up t-shirt. "He'll be back soon. Maybe I can show you around. Like I said, we're kinda new here ourselves, and—"

I peer at him. "Really? You'd let me hang with you?"

"Of course! We could even grab a bite to eat after this, maybe somewhere on the boardwalk. You don't have to be alone, y'know. I'll show you just what paradise is like."

I'm not one to cling to fleeting hope, but this sounds promising—more promising than chasing some dream with the owner of the popular beachside bar. Maybe I can make something last for a few days with this guy. "Thanks."

"No sweat." He smiles at me. "What's your name?"

I glance down at his blanket. The names of the little Pac-Man ghosts are traced along the edge in an arcade font. Inky, Blinky, Pinky, and—"Clyde," I tell him, reading the name of the little orange one.

Rule number one of getting by when you're on the run: don't *ever* use your real name.

"It's nice to meet you, Clyde! Hey, you wanna go for a little dip with me? I think I might enjoy the water one last time before the sun's gone. I see you're not in a bathing suit, but maybe you can kick off your shoes and—?"

"Nah, it's alright. You go on ahead. I just want to sit here and chill for a bit."

"You sure?"

"Yep."

"Alright. My boyfriend will be back any second. If you change your mind, you know where to find me!" He lets out a cute, silly laugh, then hops off of the blanket and heads toward the crashing waves.

I glance at the things he left behind. The blanket. An empty orange cooler with an opened can of Mountain Dew next to it. His shades. A crumpled-up t-shirt.

And peeking out from under that t-shirt: a wallet.

I bite my lip. I won't steal again. I won't steal again. I won't—*Fuck.*

The next second, I've got his wallet in hand, and thirty bucks goes missing. I leave the credit card and everything else, because I'm not a total idiot. He may not even realize he's missing the cash until he gets home or goes out to eat; he'll just think I got bored and took off. What do I owe him anyway? I pocket the cash and hurry to my feet, trying my best to be quick but also discreet. No one's eyes are on me as I head off, making my way up the beach to the road.

Maybe this is why I have no friends.

I always prioritize instant rewards over long games.

But how am I expected to be any different? Nothing good lasts. Every single promise ever made to me has been broken my whole damned life. I'm fairly certain this place is paradise only for everyone else. Less privileged guys like me don't deserve a slice of it. We're left to fend for ourselves among the scraps left behind by all of the more fortunate and lucky in life. Guys like me have to take what we can get, then scram. Even if it means being lonely.

I sit on the curb, hidden slightly by a thicket of trees at

my back. The briny air blows across my face as cars drift by, their occupants oblivious to life's problems and happy as can be. I gnaw on my lip as I fiddle with the cash in my pocket, wondering what I should do with it. Tourist spots aren't exactly the most efficient way to stretch your money, with everything so exorbitantly marked up and expensive. I have to hit up a cheapo gas station with fixed prices, or else find a spot on the northwest end of the island where the locals hang. Venturing into locals' territory has its risks.

Every moment of my life lately is riddled with risks.

Maybe I should've trusted that nice young guy to take me out for a meal. But it always goes down the same: some well-meaning person tries to help me, learns I'm homeless, boyfriend gets suspicious, then I'm back on the streets. No matter how nice people are, they never follow through.

I've likely burned my chances at the beach for another weekend or so. The shirt I'm wearing was snatched from a hot dude two weekends ago, and my shoes, from someone just the other day. I have to wait for this rush of tourists to turn over to a new crowd before I start exploring again, but with it being Pride week, that may prove difficult.

I wish Cooper hadn't caught me. It's never a good idea to piss off the locals. *Will I ever end this cycle of stealing?*

"Finders keepers, right?"

I flinch, startled, and turn around.

Speak of the fucking nut devil.

CHAPTER 4

COOPER

I HAVE TO ADMIT, HE LOOKS CUTE WHEN HE'S CAUGHT.

"Don't run," I tell him the second he moves. "I'm not gonna chase after you or call the police."

To my surprise, the boy actually stops and stares at me, staying right in place.

Hmm, that wasn't expected.

"But I will, however, encourage you to give back what you stole," I go on.

His pretty face twists with a frown. "Stole?"

"You heard me."

"I didn't steal anything."

I roll my eyes. "Really? You're gonna play dumb with me? We're gonna do this song and dance?"

He shrugs defiantly. "You must be mixing me up with some other guy."

"You've been stealing from my bar. Multiple times."

"Oh, is that what you're talking about?" he asks as he lifts his eyebrows in mock surprise, his forehead wrinkling up adorably. "I didn't steal anything, sir. The nuts were out on the table for anyone. They're free."

"Not that full-ass can you had in your hand, which you could have only gotten from my inventory room. And not to mention a twelve-pack of Pepsi, which you also took."

"I don't know what you're talking about."

"Oh, I think you do."

"I can outrun you, y'know."

This kid sure is pretty damned cocky. "Yeah, sure you can, but you can't outrun whatever you think you're gettin' away with. Someday, it's all gonna catch up to you, and it's better it happens now with me than while sittin' behind bars in a county jail, I can promise you that."

We're squared off on the side of Boardwalk Street with a good ten or twelve feet between us. The sun has crept far enough down the sky to turn the streetlights on.

If he runs now, I may lose him for good.

But the longer I look into his eyes, the less sure I am about why I'm here. Is it really about stolen snacks?

There's a story behind this boy's eyes. A troubling story. Is he just some brat burning time while his parents enjoy the island? Or is this a runaway situation? What am I facing here?

"Do you need food?" I ask a touch more sensitively. "Are your parents being dicks? You on the run? Tell me what's going on with you."

"Fuck my parents. I'm eighteen. They don't control me or tell me what to do."

Ah, the new-adult confidence of an eighteen-year-old. I can remember that feeling like it was yesterday. "Hey, I'm just making sure you're alright."

"I'll worry about myself," he says, taking a step back. "You can just fuck off."

"That's not the way you speak to the guy whose nuts you've been stealing."

"I don't know what you're—"

"You obviously like my nuts. You keep getting your hands on them. You like my nuts, boy?" I take another step toward him. "You want more of my nuts?"

He blushes, annoyed. "Stop saying 'nuts' like that."

"So what's your deal, then? You have nowhere to stay tonight? Are you living on the streets? Tell me something I can believe. Anything." The guy stays silent and defiant. I let out a patient sigh. "Look, kid … you can continue doing whatever it is you want to do out here in Dreamwood, keep robbing people, stirring up shit on the beach … or …"

I stare at his eyes, his sweet and troubled eyes. And his hair, a total mess, in need of a serious, decent shower. His oversized t-shirt, stained in places, and his balled-up fists, looking ready to fend off a family of hungry tigers for a morsel. The soft blush of his cheeks, which don't have a hair on them. His pouty, parted lips.

Is this part of his game? Making me feel an instant and unrelenting responsibility to take care of him? Waking up a dormant need in me to protect something precious? Just the way he looks at me rips my heart right out of my chest.

I literally can't leave him alone like this. I don't know the first thing about him, and all I want to do is nurture him. *Maybe I'm the one who's messed up.*

"Or … let me help you out," I finish.

He lets out a breath. "Help me?"

"Yeah. I can help. You're out here by yourself, right? You're obviously stealing for a reason. Let me help you."

He doesn't move. I figure he's trying to decide whether or not to trust me. If he really is on the run from something, I sure as hell don't blame him for questioning any and all acts of kindness. He's probably been betrayed before. Hurt.

Taken advantage of.

It makes me seethe, to think of it.

"Makes no difference to me," I go on, trying not to go soft on him too quickly. "Whether you're visiting here with some high school friends, or your parents, or a boyfriend who's treating you wrong ... or if you really are all alone, on the run from something you don't feel like disclosing. All fine. Don't need to tell me. But you don't have to steal anything anymore. No one here deserves to be stolen from. We look out for our own. I'll help you."

"Our own ...?" He snorts. "I'm not one of you."

"You could be."

His eyebrows pinch together cynically. Then he drops his gaze to the ground, and for a second, I swear all of his walls fall straight down, exposing the real him.

He's scared. He's alone. He needs protecting and being taken care of. He worries from meal to meal. He watches his back. He can't sleep a full night.

I can protect him. I can take care of him. All I need is for him to see that.

"I can see it in your eyes," I tell him. "You're just ... looking for a home. Maybe you're already here."

He doesn't say anything. He doesn't look up from the ground. He doesn't even move.

I could be the one who's full of delusions here. Some people, they don't care how much niceness and kindness you exhibit; they will never trust you, like you, or change.

I know when enough is enough. "Alright. I'll leave you be, then. The bar is busy anyway, and I kinda stranded my staff to come find you. But no worries. No one cares when

I sacrifice my time for them. Have a lovely night out here, whoever you are." I turn around and head away.

One and a half blocks later, I notice he's following me.

I smirk and come to a stop, glancing over my shoulder. "Changed your mind?"

He frowns. "No."

"You saying you want my help?"

"I'm not saying I do."

"You're not saying you don't, either."

He thrusts his hands into his pockets, annoyed.

I turn to face him completely. "Look, I've got a lot of hookups and people who owe me favors all over the island. It isn't a problem. I could easily get you a free room at the Sunnyview up by the pier. Free breakfasts included. A bed. Shower. TV. Fluffy towels and pillows. That sound nice?"

He lifts his adorable eyes to mine and says nothing.

I take that as his way of saying yes. "Come with me. It's up this street a few blocks."

I take a sharp turn and make my way. He follows some distance behind me, understandably guarded. It'll take a lot of time for him to trust me, but that's okay; as long as he's with me, he's off the streets.

When we reach the Sunnyview, however, I'm less than happy with my buddy Taj's reply at the front desk: "I'm *so* sorry, Coop, but I can't swing anything this weekend. All of the rooms are booked. Even the economy ones."

"Even the economy—?" I huff, frustrated. "What about the sister motel next door?"

"Same problem. We actually had to send our overflow to them. It's *packed* with all the Pride stuff going on. Plus everyone here's hooked up with tickets to the Hopewell Fair thanks to Marty. Can't budge, no vacancies." He pouts dramatically, looking as if he might break down into tears. He always gets overly upset when he can't help me out.

I nod slowly and pat his shoulder. "It's okay. No sweat. I can still hit up the Elysian."

"Sure, but you'll probably run into the same issue." He notices my companion for the first time, and his whole face changes. "Oh ... You're entertaining someone tonight. I ... I understand the urgency now. You need a *room*-room."

I peer back at the kid—who returns a blank, uncertain expression—then snort at my friend, shaking my head. "No way, no, no, that's not what this is." I nearly laugh. "I'm just ... helping out an acquaintance."

"You sure?" Taj bites his lip, studying him. "He's *cute*. I've never actually seen you with anyone, come to think of it. This is much more of an *Adrian* move, really."

I pat Taj more vigorously. "Okay, thanks, appreciate it, gonna go try another hotel."

"Good luck," he says distractedly, staring at the kid.

We depart the Sunnyview and head on down the road, though I've got a lot less energy in my walk. I was almost certain I could've hooked him up at the Sunnyview, which always has at least one or two spare rooms for emergencies or unanticipated overflow. Hell, I've heard the owner even keeps a room set aside for "specific sexual interests" of his own, which I only know about because everyone tells me every damned thing that goes on around the island. Being the main focal point of all gossip around here has its perks.

But that doesn't bring me any closer to helping out my new acquaintance here.

Speaking of: "So what do I call you?" I ask him. "I can just keep callin' you 'kid', but that's gonna feel weird after a while."

He doesn't answer right away. But when he does, his eyes turn soft and thoughtful: "Sunny," he decides.

That's a burner name if I've ever heard one. Or he was inspired by the unhelpful place we just left. "Sunny, okay. We'll go with that alias for now."

"It's my real name."

No, it isn't. "It's alright. I understand you're protecting yourself. That's important. I'll call you Sunny. I'm Cooper, but I suspect you already knew that."

"Yep."

"You gonna tell me yet what brought you out here to Dreamwood? Or do I have to keep prying and fishing?" He doesn't answer. "Prying and fishing it is."

"No one's gonna have a free room, y'know."

34

"People owe me favors," I remind him, "and I—"

"Obviously they don't owe you enough to actually pay. You heard your so-called 'buddy' at the Sunnyview place. No one's just gonna hand you over a free room when that room can be paid for by some big happy family with deep pockets. It's just bad business."

And now this cute, cocky kid is gonna school me about business practices? "We'll see about a spot at the Elysian. I know the general manager."

"Isn't that even pricier and fancier than Sunnyview?"

"Let *me* worry about the pricy and fancy," I sass back.

But when we reach the Elysian Seaside Resort & Spa, just across the street from the boardwalk, I'm met with the same damned resistance from my friend Armando, general manager of the place. "This is truly a week like none other," he says in his soft yet authoritative drawl, lightly accented, his heavy-lidded eyes blinking apologetically at me. "Just got off of the phone with Luke, even El Amado is at max capacity. Are you not swamped at your bar tonight? I would imagine you'd be quite busy. Too busy to be …" His eyes fall on Sunny. "… entertaining company."

I lean in close and bring my voice down. "He's not just a guy I picked up. He's in a situation. He needs a room."

"A situation? Now you make things interesting."

"I just want to help him out, alright? Get him off of the streets for a night."

Armando clicks his tongue and shakes his head. "Truly I'm sorry. I fear I don't even have a *storage closet* for the poor soul. Have you tried the Hopewell's? They must have fifteen bedrooms in that mansion of theirs off the pier."

My patience is wearing thin. "I've stretched Finn and his dad's resources enough. Besides, they're busy with all the extra Pride stuff this weekend."

"Wasn't that last weekend?"

"It's *every* weekend," I mutter, and to that, Armando rolls his eyes and says, "Touché."

I don't get any farther with him than that.

We sit on the edge of a short concrete wall outside the Elysian, staring out at the beach and the boardwalk across the street, the small L-shape of my Easy Breezy bar in the distance. It's dark now, and I am no closer to getting this poor kid off the street than I was when I was just chasing him across the sand over a can of peanuts.

"I've still got my spot in the park."

I lift an eyebrow at him. "What? You're not sleeping in the park."

"It's handy. Near everything. Well, there's the issue of dealing with the twitchy weirdo who acts like he's my new best friend, always trying to get me to tweak out with him and won't leave me alone. But I can deal with him. I found a pizza thrown away in the movie theater dumpster once, still in its box, totally untouched. Tourists are wasteful."

I don't know what to do. I'm running out of options.

"Look, I don't need your money," he says, "or ... or whatever it is you're doing. I can take care of myself."

"I'm sure you can as you obviously have up 'til now," I say less than patiently, "but the difference between you taking care of yourself and me giving you a hand is you having a decent meal in your belly and a roof over your head ... instead of secondhand pizza, druggies harassing you in the park, and flies biting your butt."

He scrunches up his face. "Flies doing *what* now?"

"You heard me. Sleep in that park long enough, flies are gonna swarm and bite your butt in your sleep."

"Flies don't bite."

"But if you enjoy flies biting your butt and eating pizza out of a dumpster, be my guest."

"Well, what other options do I have?"

I gnaw on my lip, staring across the road and the sand, at the quaint, friendly shape of the Easy Breezy.

The only option that's left is the very last one.

The one I was trying to avoid.

I hop off the wall. "You hungry? My bar is still open. If you prefer dumpster diving, that's your prerogative. But if you come with me, I've got chicken wings, nachos, and all the damned nuts you want. The difference this time is I'm actually *offerin'* you the food, on the house."

"The nuts were free. They were on every table."

That's a battle I won't win. "C'mon, *Sunny*. I'm pretty sure all of this chasing around town has worked you up an appetite. I won't take no for an answer."

For the first time, he doesn't fight me on it.

The bar is just as busy and out of control as my worst nightmare would have revealed. Adrian is long gone, and Mars and Chase are scrambling behind the counter to keep up with the customers. Sweat drips from their brows. Even August our cook is delivering drinks to customers all over the room, his apron stained with three different sauces.

Easy Breezy is anything *but* easy and breezy tonight.

I head behind the counter and grab hold of the reins, sending Mars to the floor and August back to the kitchen. The kid hangs around in the back by the windows, his big bright eyes scanning the room guardedly.

In ten minutes, he's got a hot basket of chicken wings, fries, and nachos which, between customers, I observe him devouring. Despite us being slammed by the business, just the satisfied, grateful, overjoyed look on his face as he eats is enough payment for everything.

And as the crowd starts to ebb near midnight, Mars at last gets a chance to nudge up next to me at the bar, her eyes on the boy. "You really think that's a good idea?"

I glance at her. "What do you mean?"

"Indulging in this ... *thief* kid you don't know the first thing about."

"I know he isn't dangerous," I tell her. "I know he just needs a little help. Place to stay. Food in his belly. I can't just leave him on a weekend as busy as this. Who knows what kind of people are around here? Horny guys who will take advantage of him. Drunk guys who lose their sense. I don't want to risk him being around any of that."

Mars gives me a baffled look. "You're talking like that guy is some struggling lost nephew of yours you've known all of your life. Do I have to keep repeating myself, Coop? You don't know him. *At all.*"

He's licking his fingers. I smirk. "I know he's hungry."

Mars rolls her eyes. "You and your *daddy complex.*"

I give her a look. "It isn't my fault the boys flock to me. And I happen to be good at looking out for them."

"Well, someone needs to look out for *you*, Coop. I do remember the last one, y'know."

That stops me. "The last one?"

"I was too young to really get what was going on, but I heard all about it from my mom. That one young guy you took under your wing a while back ... the one who took advantage of you and ended up breaking your heart. He was about the same age, too."

I haven't given him a thought in years. "Marcia ..."

"I'm just saying. I don't want to see you hurt again. You're too nice sometimes. You don't see how harsh and cruel the world can be."

Really? She's half my age and going to teach me about the cruelty of the world? "He's just a down-on-his-luck kid who has nowhere safe to stay tonight, Mars," I point out. "If I judge everyone I meet after one bad seed, how is that fair? This kid needs my help. Doesn't matter that I don't know his story yet."

"Well, you'd better learn it fast before you go inviting him into your home and he robs you blind."

"I'm not taking him to my house. I'm gonna ... I'm gonna figure something out for him." I keep gazing at the boy from across the room, struggling to work a solution out in my head. "I just need to think."

I'm still telling myself that an hour later when the bar is officially calm again, and Chase tells me he can close up later on if I want to head off now. The kid still lingers in the back at an empty table, picking at a loose thread on his shirt and staring out the window.

I hope I don't regret this.

CHAPTER 5

SEANY

IS TONIGHT MY LUCKIEST NIGHT, OR IS THIS A TRAP?

His house is cozy to say the least. It immediately opens to a tiny kitchen area on the right and a living room straight ahead, with a couch and coffee table on one side, and a TV on the wall opposite from it. Past the couch, a sliding glass door opens to a small lit porch and the beach beyond.

"I'll get you a few things and set up the couch." He heads down the short hallway, where I guess the bedroom and bathroom are. After a moment in the bathroom, Cooper heads to a coat closet in the hallway, where he fetches a set of sheets and a pillow. "Go ahead, get settled in."

He's really gonna let me stay here? "Okay."

"I have soda and water in the fridge. Make yourself at home, but keep your hands off the beer."

I make a face. "Beer's nasty."

He brings the sheets and pillow to the couch in silence. After shifting the coffee table aside, he tosses the cushions off the couch, then pulls the whole thing open to a full bed, where he starts to fit the sheets.

I stand awkwardly to the side, watching. I'm surprised by the size of the fold-out couch. Is this even real? If I start to panic, I can still take off before sunrise. I've got a full belly and thirty bucks in my pocket.

But watching the tireless way in which Coop makes the bed, even after a stressful night working at the bar, makes me feel guilty for even considering fleeing.

What if this is the real deal?

Older men claimed to want to help me in the past. But in the end, every so-called nice guy had ulterior motives.

They wanted something in return—something I'd best provide with my clothes on the floor and my ass in the air.

And here Coop goes, setting me up a place to sleep on the couch. He isn't inviting me to his bed. In fact, after all of his efforts in trying to find me a hotel room of my own, I get the sense setting me up in his own house was his very last resort. This is not part of some devious plan.

He doesn't want me here.

"There," he says when he finishes, tossing a freshly-covered pillow onto the fold-out bed. "Place to sleep. TV if you can't. Remote's on the coffee table. Fridge if you need a drink. Got apple juice also. Crackers in the cupboard."

Crackers in the cupboard? Are those animal crackers? Is he about to offer me a juice box, too?

I feel like the ten-year-old he's babysitting.

"Thanks," I say anyway.

"If you need a shower, bathroom's down the hall." He rubs his head. "I need to finish up some work stuff before I nod off. Paperwork stuff. I'll be in my room if you need anything." He starts to head off.

"I won't be here long."

He stops and turns. "Hmm?"

"I ..." Why am I already planning my escape route? I can't let go of old habits, apparently. "I just meant I won't be, uh ... I won't be a big inconvenience or anything. I just need to get the okay to come back home, then I'm gone."

He appears confused for a second.

Did I just contradict my story with that statement?

I ramble on. "I-It's my dad. There's problems at home. That's why I ... That's why I left. Once I get the okay from my mom, then I'll be out of your hair. Promise."

"Problems with your dad?"

Am I overthinking this? Do I not need this stupid story to keep him on the hook? *Why can't I just be honest?*

"I ... I don't want to talk about it."

After a moment, he nods. "Alright. So ... you've got a phone? They're gonna call you or something?"

"Not anymore. I ..." My phone was stolen back in San Antonio. This story is getting too complicated. "I check in every now and then with my mom, that's it. At a ... a gas station. Or wherever I can. Just to see if the coast is clear."

He frowns in thought. "And how long have you been waiting for that coast to clear?"

I avert my eyes and continue to hug myself, standing there like a ghoul. I'm out of stories to fudge together. Out of steam. Out of everything.

I'm so sick of lying.

"I don't need to know the whole story if you don't feel comfortable sharing it," he says suddenly. "We can figure out something tomorrow. A better situation for you. Maybe the hotels will free up after the weekend. I can get you a room of your own, just 'til you're back on your feet."

Back on my feet. What a concept.

A fucking pipedream, more like.

He spends a minute studying my silence, as if waiting for whether I have anything to say, then gives an indistinct grunt before dismissing himself to his room down the hall. His door is left open. Lamplight spills out when I hear a faint click, then the noise of soft tapping at a computer as he gets to work, I presume.

44

I hurry to the bathroom, shut the door, and lock it. A feeling of safety enwraps me, despite my drumming heart. A towel with pastel dots and stripes hangs on the rack next to a lime green washcloth. A pair of baby blue gym shorts, a plain white t-shirt, and gray Hilfiger boxer-briefs sit folded on the counter by the sink. None of them look like they've been worn before, or else they're just super clean. On top is a brand-new toothbrush still in its package.

I guess he left these for me.

I don't know how to feel about that yet.

The bathroom has a lone window over the toilet, which is comforting. *There's always an easy way out, if I need it.* After a moment's hesitation, I strip down to nothing, then twist on the water. The shower is a tiled stall, gray and white in color, marbled, with a glass door. Once the water is warm enough to fog up the glass, I step in, then nearly moan as the water pours over me, the temperature perfect.

I can't remember the last time I had a shower in an actual shower. It's a little glass box of heaven. Warm, safe, all to myself. Nothing scary to watch for over my back.

I grab the bar of soap and lather up. Next to the soap dish sits a bottle of combo shampoo and conditioner, which I squirt way too much of atop my head. It smells exactly like Coop. A smile spreads over my face as I stand under the steamy, plentiful water, giddy from the experience of feeling all of these soapsuds and fragrant fluids running down my skin, caressing and embracing me.

Then I cry.

The steam hugs me like it's trying to console me. The water keeps pouring over my head, the white noise filling my ears.

And I cry some more.

It's weird, to think that just this morning, I was certain my life would never feel normal again.

I must spend a full hour in this safe little glass box. When I shut the water off, I step out in a relaxing cloud of steam and relief, then wrap the towel around my waist.

That's when the safe feeling starts to fade. I was okay in here, all by myself, but I'm going to have to leave the bathroom eventually, aren't I? I glance at the shirt, shorts, and boxer-briefs again, reluctant. Putting them on suddenly feels like a contract I'm signing. I glance back at the door, gnawing on my lip uncertainly.

Maybe I don't have to leave the bathroom just yet.

Cooper is a nice man. A good man. Generous. Forgives easily. Even after I brazenly stole from him, he invited me back to his bar and fed me. Now I'm in his house, still wet from his shower, and smelling like a million bucks.

And I still don't sense anything weird about him.

Can I really trust this?

All of the instincts that are telling me to relax are the same ones that won't let me. My gut has never been wrong about guys before—but it's also never been this confused. I can't even tell if the clothes on this counter are a gesture of kindness or just another mousetrap waiting to snap the second I get those Hilfiger undies hugging my nuts.

Cooper doesn't seem like a bad man.

I'm the only one between us who's done any bad. He's only been good to me. He didn't even call the cops.

And he's good-looking—way better looking than I first realized scouting him out from a distance in the back of the bar, hiding like a shadow.

Maybe I'm confused right now because he's one of the first gay men I've met who I wouldn't be opposed to being intimate with. Not that the man's offering. In fact, that seems to be the last damned thing on his mind.

Still, I can't ignore it. Cooper is a handsome man. And the subtle flecks of gray in his temples, added with the way his eyes sharply take in everything they see, gives him a classy, solid maturity that makes me feel safe around him, like he has the answer to everything, like no harm can come to me if I stay around him. I find that very appealing, present circumstances considered.

That's not all I find appealing.

I can tell he's muscled underneath his clothes, which don't hide his impressive physique that well. In certain light, such as at the bar, you can even count his abs through his shirt when it clings to him in the right way. His poor sleeves suffer every tiny movement of his big, strong arms, which I can't help but imagine wrapped tightly around me, holding me close to his broad, muscled chest, protecting me from the dangerous world out there.

He's easy to trust.

That's also why he terrifies me.

Do I actually like him in that way? That has to be why I stuck around this long without bolting. Or why I trusted his acts of kindness when he took me to his bar to enjoy way more food than I deserved. It didn't even occur to me until now that he could've drugged the food if he wanted and had his nasty way with me or done something terrible. I certainly didn't see the food being made. Rookie mistake.

I trusted him blindly. And that blind trust paid off. It's why I'm in his house right now, fresh from the first shower I've had in ages, rejuvenated beyond words.

Is this really the first time something can be too good to be true—and still be true?

I unlock the bathroom door, then glance out of it. I can still hear the soft tapping of computer keys from his room. I quietly step into the hall, then come to the edge of his doorway, peering inside. He's at a desk in the corner of the room by a large window, which shows the back porch and the beach, with a laptop opened in front of him next to a lamp. His bed is twice the size of the couch and seems as comfy as a cloud.

He senses me and looks over.

His eyes drop to my bare wet chest where they linger for a second, as if caught in a spider's web.

Why does that tiny shift of his eyes to my chest make my heart race excitedly?

The next instant, he snaps his gaze away. "Those clothes I left folded up on the counter were for you. They should fit you better than the ones you had. Plus, they're clean. They're all yours."

I bite my lip, studying his expression. "I'm just cooling off. Can't I cool off for a bit?"

"Of course. Take your time. I'm just ..." After another glance at my chest, he makes a halfhearted gesture at his computer. "... working."

I liked the way he looked at me just now. When I know I've got a guy's figurative balls in my grip, I feel more in control. I feel safer—*assuming I don't tease said balls too much and find my head in the lion's mouth.*

Maybe I shouldn't press that button too quickly; it isn't wise to count my sheep before I've actually got them.

"Need anything else?" he asks, typing away.

"No, sir," I say.

Then I blink.

Sir ...?

Did "sir" just seriously come out of my mouth?

His typing stops. "If you need anything else, *Sunny*,

then just let me know. I'll be going to bed soon."

"Me, too."

He nods, then returns to his work.

I wander back to the living room. Through the sliding back door, I can see distant waves crashing on the shore, lit only by the sparkle of the moon's light shattering over the water and causing the wet sand to glow, bright and crystalline. The breeze stirs a wooden wind chime hanging on the porch, which clanks and rattles musically. I watch it, the air of the living room feeling cold and crisp against my damp, exposed skin.

I'm so far from sleep right now.

Quietly, I return to his doorway and peek in. He closed his laptop and is pinching the bridge of his nose, eyes shut, looking troubled. I watch him for a moment as he just sits there, motionless except for the subtle rising and falling of his chest as he breathes.

I'm slowly getting the sense Cooper is a complex man. Everyone on the island knows him, but he lives alone. His bar is his pride and joy, he seems financially stable, has a nice roof over his head, yet looks unsatisfied somehow.

I wonder if anyone truly knows Cooper.

The moment he lifts his head, I vanish from sight, then slip back into the bathroom. The clothes he offered are still there, folded neatly, awaiting me.

It's so easy *and* difficult to accept help.

Fuck it.

I take off the towel and hang it on the rack to dry. Then I pull on the gray boxer-briefs, followed by the blue shorts, and finally I tug the white t-shirt over my head. The shirt is a little snug at the pits, but it fits good otherwise. I gaze at myself in the mirror for a moment, then stare down at the clothes I took off earlier. I rummage through them, fish out the thirty bucks, and shove the cash into my new shorts. I consider the rest of my dirty clothes piled atop my shoes, unsure what to do with them. Gathering them up, I take the pile out to the couch, where I tuck them under the pull-out, then sit on the mattress next to them like a guard dog.

The silence of the room fills my ears.

I hear footsteps. Cooper appears in the hall. "I'm gonna take a quick shower. You need anything before I go in?"

I look at him, startled. His face is so handsome when he looks all serious like that, his eyebrows pulled together and his jaw set tightly, causing dimples to appear in his cheeks. His frame is so broad and powerful-looking, I have to admit it's difficult not to think things while he looks at me that way.

It's been a long time since I've been touched. Even just to be held. Comforted. Even longer since I had someone I cared about stroke my hair or caress me, let alone kiss me.

I would let him caress me.

I would let him kiss me.

"I don't have to worry, do I?" he asks suddenly.

I flinch, taken aback. "Worry?"

"While I'm in the shower."

"I …" Oh. He means whether or not I'm going to steal everything in his house and take off running to the nearest pawn shop. "N-No, sir. I don't plan to steal a damned—"

Huh? For fuck's sake, with that "sir" thing again!

I blink away the annoying formality and fight back my blushing cheeks. "No. I'm not a—" Well, I can't say I'm not a thief, now can I? That part's been more or less proven as dead false. Everything I was wearing before my shower is something I stole. "I'm not a bad—" How can I claim to be a good person after what I've done? I sigh and settle on something more honest. "I … have nowhere else to go."

He studies me a while longer. He says nothing.

I stare at the wooden trinket as it dances in the wind. "You've been nice to me. You gave me so much already. I've got no reason to take anything more from you."

"You have every reason."

I look back at him.

He sighs. "But … I'm gonna trust you anyway, Sunny. That's something else I'm giving you … something that can't be held in your hands, yet can easily be broken all the same. I'm giving you my trust."

Something inside me gives.

The look in his eyes.

The pain and lonesomeness that seems to match mine.

The soul I know is hidden deep inside him.

And that's when I decide to play my most closely-held card for the first time since I left home: "I-It's Seany."

He meets my eyes, confused. "Huh?"

"My name. My ... real name." I swallow hard, keeping my steady gaze on his. "My name's Seany."

His face softens as he looks me over, curious. He gives me a gentler nod. "Seany." His jaw tightens. "I'll be back in a minute ... Seany." Then he heads off to the bathroom. I listen as the door gently shuts, then the water turns on.

CHAPTER 6

I ONLY WANTED TO GIVE HIM MY TRUST.

Then he gives me his trust right back, revealing his real name to me. That's something I can damned well guarantee he hasn't done in a very long time.

Seany.

Assuming that *is* his real name.

I'll admit, despite the little mutual trust-giving, I take a much shorter shower than I usually do and dry off in record speed. After putting on some loose sweatpants and a tank, I come out of the bathroom to find Seany lying on the couch bed with the TV on, remote balanced on his stomach.

He glances my way, then sits up at once. The remote slides off his stomach and drops to the mattress.

"It's okay, you can relax," I assure him before heading to the fridge to pull out a beer. He watches me. "You want anything? Drink? Late-night snack?"

"No, I'm fine," he says, still watching me like I might lash out at him with a weapon at any second.

That look of unrelenting caution in his eyes kills me. I wish I could put him at ease somehow. "If you change your mind ..." I shut the fridge, crack open my beer, then take a sip. Some game show is on TV. "What's this? *Press Your Luck*? Thought that oldie ended ages ago."

"The streets of San Antonio were scary."

His somber tone changes me. I set down my beer and come around the counter, forgetting it instantly. "Scary?"

"Couldn't do the Riverwalk. Too many homeless. A guy with tons of tattoos was armed with a stolen Saltgrass steak knife defending his spot under the bridge like he owned it. I called him the Tatted Troll." Seany lifts his arm and points at a jagged scar running across it in the shape of a warped boomerang. "Earned me this lovely keepsake. I learned that night just how fast my heart can beat without exploding in my chest."

"That sounds terrible."

"Well, that's not the worst." He looks away. "Anyway, caught a ride on the bus and happened upon this place ...

Dreamwood Isle, thinking this would be paradise, but …"
He shakes his head. "I guess my head's still in the clouds.
It's what Dad always said. I'm full of childish dreams …
all swimming around in my head. I needed to be realistic. I
needed to have goals."

I get the fast impression his dad isn't a great man. He
didn't want to talk about him before. "Your dad …?"

"Don't wanna talk 'bout it."

Still a hot topic. I won't pry further. "Dreamwood isn't
all that bad," I tell him, shifting gears. "Maybe you … just
caught us at a bad time. We're pretty welcoming, actually."

"Yeah, if you're horny and got deep pockets."

I shrug. "Well, it *is* a tourist spot. But that's just half of
it—the half most of us locals depend on to survive."

"But what about me? I'm not a tourist *or* a local."

"You're my guest, that's what."

He runs his finger along his scar in thought, then lifts
his eyes to me. "So what happens tomorrow? When the sun
is up, it's a new day, and your kindness runs dry? Gonna
turn me out onto the streets again? I'll understand, but … I
just want to know if I should be ready for that."

He's already talking about leaving. I wonder when was
the last time he's had a reliable place to stay. How long has
he been sleeping with one eye open? "I run a bar," I tease
him with a smirk. "Nothing about me ever runs dry."

He gazes downward in silence.

This isn't going to be a quick thing.

I'm realizing that fast.

What he needs is stability. Reliability. Consistency. He needs transparency, too. He needs the version of me that has no walls up.

Make it or break it, Coop.

I turn serious. "Look, Seany, this arrangement doesn't have an expiration date. Come the morning, you can stay right here if you want."

He meets my eyes. "Really?"

"Yep. Really. I mean, I *was* serious about rechecking the hotels at the end of the weekend, in case you would like your own space, somewhere to feel safe, in control of your life, whatever you need." I furrow my brow and nod. "I don't break a promise."

He picks at his fingers and averts his gaze.

I take a breath. "However much time you need to stay here, I understand. I opened my doors to you, and the only person who can shut them is you. All I ask in return is that we trust each other. That's it. Nothing more."

He mulls that over. "Seems reasonable."

"So can we do that? … Can we trust each other?"

"Yeah." He looks at me with sweet yet heavy eyes, full of sadness and uncertainty. "Thank you."

Thank you, he says.

I almost can't bear it, the pain on his face.

I can't imagine what he's endured out there. I doubt that little scar on his arm is all he has to show for it. What about the scars that can't be seen with the eyes? The ones on his soul, on his confidence, on his pride?

He's too young to have suffered wounds like that.

"I'll leave you be," I decide rather abruptly, getting to my feet. "You've had a long day. No doubt you want to get some serious sleep. Get your rest. I'm just down the hall if you need anything."

"Okay."

After a moment's hesitation, I head down the hall. I've forgotten about my opened beer I left on the counter by the time I drop onto my bed and shut my eyes. It's well past three at this point. Maybe four. The night's gone on long enough. It's about time it comes to a damned end already.

But no sleep finds me.

I'm wide fucking awake.

I can wax poetic for an hour about trust this and trust that, but what do words get you when a person who is truly desperate to survive reaches a breaking point? I can look at his sweet, youthful eyes, be charmed, and offer him a bed for a night or two, but do I really know the first thing about him? How many other older, lonely men has he charmed in his time on the streets? Who else's bed has he slept in?

Can I really trust him as much as I expect him to trust me? Was it even fair to ask that of him?

I notice the TV in the living room has turned off. In the still silence, every noise in the house touches my ears like an explosion. Each time the wind picks up off the beach. Each time my wood chimes rattle on the back porch. Each time the windows shudder, or the walls settle, or the couch creaks under Seany's shifting weight. Sleep won't find me.

Then I hear the soft padding of feet.

Closer.

Closer still.

His silhouette appears at my bedroom door. I watch him through the dark, unsure if he can see my eyes open. He stands there and says nothing, one hand hanging by his side, one clinging to the doorframe. He seems uncertain. Or curious. Or just as cautious as I am.

Then: "Coop?"

I lift my head off of the pillow. "Something wrong?"

"No." He shuffles by the door, then folds his arms. "I just can't sleep. Sorry."

"It's alright. Me neither. Wanna chat a bit? Get some stuff off your mind?"

"We don't have enough time in the world to do that."

I think he's trying for a joke. I indulge him with a dry chuckle, then sit up all the way and slide to the edge of the bed. "We can stay up a little longer. Watch some TV until we're tired. How does that sound?"

"I don't know if I feel like doing that."

"Okay. We could …" Am I supposed to read his mind here? "We could pop some popcorn. Hot chocolate. Sit out on the porch and listen to the ocean. I think I've got some sugar-free popsicles in the freezer."

"Those sound gross."

"Leftovers from a party at the Hopewells'. No one else wanted them. I like something sweet now and then."

"Why do you keep trying to feed me?"

"Just brainstormin' here. When I have trouble sleeping, sometimes a light snack does the trick."

"I'm not hungry."

"What do you want to do then?"

"I don't know."

The silence of the house presses against us like the walls themselves are closing in. I swear I can hear his heart beating from across the room. Or is that my own?

I shrug. "We could just … sit here and do nothing, if you prefer."

He doesn't say anything. Slowly, he shuffles into the room and sits on the other end of the bed, his arms still crossed. The room falls silent again.

I don't know what to say. Or ask. Or do.

Perhaps the point is to say nothing, ask nothing, and do nothing.

This isn't how I problem-solve. I always take action. I do things. I count inventory and seek errors. I connect with customers at the bar every night and figure out how to make them happy. I listen to friends' problems and work out solutions they can't see themselves. I'm a fixer.

But there's no way to fix this.

Especially when I only know a fraction of the problem.

Sitting still is fucking agony.

"Thanks," he says softly.

I turn to him. In the dark, we're both just silhouettes. I could be anyone. He could be anyone. The only thing we know about each other anymore is the sound of our breaths as they drift in, then let out.

I feel strangely close to him.

Connected by this wild, interesting night we've shared.

"I don't know if I can sleep out there," he volunteers rather suddenly. "I appreciate it and all, but ..."

"What do you mean?"

"I-I just ..." He goes quiet.

"Is the couch uncomfortable? A friend crashed here not too long ago. Late night. Didn't have any complaints. Got the best sleep of his life on that thing, actually."

"No. It's fine. It's just ... I ..." I hear him draw a deep, long breath. "I've been on my own. For, like, so long. It ... It feels ... strange to be around someone again. To ... be in someone's house. I can't quite relax. It feels like ..."

He goes quiet again.

I can imagine a dozen things it feels like.

"Well ..." I'm unsure where is safe to tread here. "You might have some kind of idea about me by now, but ... I don't really do things like this. Ever. Letting someone I don't know sleep in my house. This is new to me, too."

"I figured at a bar like that, you get propositioned all of the time," he says.

"Of course I do. Ample opportunity to bring just about any number of guys back here if I wanted. Hell, there was a weekend I had a band of horny college boys celebrating their pal's birthday, and they were trying to rope me into a plan that involved an orgy up in the penthouse suite at the Sunnyview. But that's not really how I roll. Most of those propositions are made in total drunken lust, anyway, and who am I to take advantage of a moment of weakness? No." I shake my head, finding the mere idea ludicrous. "That's not what I want in life."

"So ... if that's not your thing ... then ..." He shifts on the bed, turning to me. "What was it about me that made you give in?"

I stare ahead. "I don't know."

"You don't know?"

"I guess I just ... couldn't imagine you on the streets. For whatever reason, you chose to come to my bar, I chose to count my inventory again, I saw something missing, and our paths crossed."

"Sounds like fate."

"Don't get ahead of yourself," I tease.

"Maybe it's more than just your inventory. Maybe you realized something else was missing."

I look at him. "What do you mean?"

"Can you hold me?"

I open my mouth to speak, then freeze at his question. *Hold him ...?* I feel Seany staring at me through the dark, across the space of bed that separates us, me at one corner, him at the other.

What did he just ask me to do?

"Please?" His voice is nearly a whimper. "I just ... feel like being held. It's been a long time. A really long time."

Is this a trick? Is this part of a bigger, more elaborate game I should have seen coming from the start?

Is he the guy with the hidden Saltgrass steak knife?

"Seany ..."

The next thing I know, he scurries across the edge of the bed and throws his arms around my waist, then nuzzles his head against my side, right under my chest, almost in my armpit. My hands are lifted in alarm, startled by his sudden embrace. I'm unsure where to put them.

"Please," he whimpers again.

He doesn't let go.

Please ...

I'm like the cliff he's hanging from. A pillow clutched during a nightmare. A blanket in the cold wilderness.

What am I supposed to do with this?

My arms gently settle, one around his back, the other resting on the arm he's got around my waist. When I touch him, he squeezes me a little tighter, clinging to me.

It's not a game. That's what I have to believe, even if it *is* a game. Even if I get duped in the end. Even if this is a big, elaborate scam he's pulled on a dozen other men as foolish and lonely as myself.

I have to take him at his word.

Because if this *isn't* a game, then he's someone who needs my help—and I think I'd rather err on the side of compassion than guarded cynicism and suspicion.

"Come here," I tell him, patting his back, as I detach from him and slide up the bed, back to where I was lying before he came in. He watches me for a second before he follows me across the bed to the pillows. I open my arms, and like a magnet, he nuzzles within them, his back against my chest. I close my arms, spooning him against my body.

The feel of another person in my arms, cuddled to my chest like a treasure, warm and safe and protected, simply doesn't compare to anything. How could I have forgotten what this feels like, to care for someone, to hold them close and feel as if I could never let them go if I wanted?

How long has it been since I held someone?

It's nearly crushing, how good this feels.

"I've been wondering this past week ... what a life out

here would be like," says Seany, his voice soft and curious. "A real one. In a house like this, for example. Waking up to the sounds of the beach every morning …"

"You get used to it."

"I don't want to get used to it. I don't want to get used to any of it. I'd want to cherish it every morning I open my eyes, like it's this big surprise … every morning I wake up, thankful for the waves crashing on the shore, thankful for the air in my lungs … thankful I'm alive."

He nuzzles back against me, his cute butt pressed to my crotch, his back glued to my chest, his legs and feet fitted around mine like we're two halves of a whole that all this time were meant to piece together perfectly, puzzle pieces locked together as one.

"That's a beautiful way to live," I remark.

We grow quiet together. Somehow, holding him in my arms does the trick. I feel safer. I feel calmer. And I feel like I'm doing whatever little part I can in healing whatever it is that hurts Seany deep down. Even if it'll take a dozen more nights like this to truly heal him. Or a hundred. Or an unknowable amount that can't possibly be quantified.

I'm certain he isn't waiting on an "okay" from home. He's been running from something. His dad. His mom. Or both of them. It doesn't matter to me. He's safe here.

I just hope he knows that.

CHAPTER 7

SEANY

I OPEN MY EYES, EXPECTING DARKNESS.

Instead, the sun beams through the window, filling the bedroom with sunlight, obscured only slightly by curtains I didn't notice last night.

The next instant, I sit up, alarmed.

I forgot where I am.

For one terrifying moment of utter oblivion, I feel like the events of last night were a wild dream that's about to shatter as the cold dread of reality makes itself known.

Then the moment passes.

I take a breath.

I'm safe.

I peer to the side and realize I'm in Cooper's bed all by myself. We never got under the sheets last night. They are disturbed by our bodies, crinkled and twisted. Over my feet is a crumpled-up blanket that might have been laid over me at some point in the night. Did Coop do that? And wasn't I facing the other way when I drifted off last night, not able to see the window?

The sound of something softly clinking in the kitchen draws my attention. A spoon in a coffee mug. Or a fork on a plate. *He's awake.* I slide off the bed and pad over to the door, then peek an eye out, peering down the hallway at the kitchen, visible from here.

Coop stands at the counter in his tight, muscle-showing tank top and gray sweatpants, which hug the globes of his butt in excruciating detail. I don't think he's wearing any underwear beneath, the way those sweatpants even seem to reveal the cleavage between his pert cheeks.

I watch, curious, as he dips something into his steamy coffee mug. Oh, it's a teabag. He turns slightly, giving me his profile, and my eyes drop to his crotch.

His ... very plentiful crotch.

Nope, definitely not wearing underwear.

As he lifts and dips the teabag in his mug of hot water over and over, I watch the bicep in his arm bulge. In the bright morning daylight, I see so much more of him, and I can confidently say, my attraction to the man was not in any way misplaced. He hides nothing unflattering in the dark; every part of him is beautiful.

And his beauty in the daylight is a bit devastating after the kind of night we had, with so much soul-baring. I felt more vulnerable last night than I had in a long time, and all Coop did was protect me—both from others *and* myself.

I fucking hope I don't scare him away.

I don't make a sound, but he looks up suddenly, maybe sensing me. "Morning."

I stay at the doorframe uncertainly. "Morning."

"Hungry? I can whip us up some eggs and toast."

My stomach immediately growls before I can answer. I guess he hears it, because he sets down his tea and gets to work pulling stuff out of the fridge. After a brief moment, I come down the hall and hover near the counter, watching as he works. I'm not sure what to say, so I say nothing.

The floodgates open over breakfast when we're eating at a tiny table on the back porch I hadn't noticed before. "These're the best fucking eggs I've ever had," I announce through my mouthful. I can't eat them fast enough.

Cooper nods. "Sure seems like it."

"How do you wake up to this view every morning and not just cry?" I ask, gesturing with my fork at the beach. "I mean, the ocean's at your back doorstep. Hop down these little wood planks and you've got sand between your toes."

"Like I said, you get used to—"

"Well, that's gonna stop right now," I say, cutting him off, which stuns him. "While I'm here, you won't be used to a damned thing anymore. I'm gonna show you what I see however I can. This house is *bomb*. These eggs are *bomb*. That fucking view is fucking *bomb*. You don't even know what you've got." I laugh, feeling manic, as I fork more eggs past my lips.

Soon we're finished, but we stay at the table, Cooper sipping his tea, me leaning back in my chair and listening to the waves.

"There's no one out there," I note.

"Sugarberry Beach," he explains. "It's quieter up here at the northwest corner of Dreamwood, away from all that noise at the south end with Breezeway Point or Quicksilver Strand—the boardwalk, the resorts, and my bar. Sometimes a few vacationers will find their way up here, but they tend to keep away. This is where us locals live."

"Can I be a local?" I settle in my chair, feeling entirely too comfortable to be real. "I feel pretty special right now."

He smirks. "Sure thing. Won't even put you through all the tough initiations we usually do to newcomers."

"Yeah, yeah, sure." I throw my hands behind my head and lean back even more. "I feel like king of the beach."

He doesn't respond. I glance over to find him gazing at me with wonder in his eyes.

I frown. "What?"

He shrugs and sets down his tea. "I was just thinking a bit about last night. Things you mentioned. I don't mean to dampen your beach vibes here ..."

Oh, fuck. I drop my hands at once. "You gotta kick me out after all?"

He quirks an eyebrow. "What? No, no. Nothing like that. The opposite, actually. Offer still stands. Stay here as long as you need, and I'll check on those hotels Monday. I was just gonna say that I ..." He glances down at his tea to gather his thoughts, then looks at me. "I hope you're okay. Truly okay. From whatever it is you're getting away from."

I don't notice my foot hopping in place, then stop it. I clear my throat. "I'm okay now. Thanks to you."

"And I know I said I wouldn't pry," he goes on, "but if there's anything I need to know, let me know, alright? ... Especially if there's something I *should* know."

I stare back at him. I can't imagine what kind of things are going through his head. All I've done is let him guess who I really am—and still he trusts me enough to let me stay here. For all he knows, I'm a criminal. Or a murderer.

Oh. I didn't think about that. "I didn't kill anyone, if that's what you're worried about."

A flash of worry tightens his face.

Whoops. That was totally the wrong thing to say. "Just meant that I, uh ... I'm not on the run from a crime. It's my dad, like I said. He's an asshole. The worst kind of asshole. The kind that even other assholes think is an asshole. I … I had to get away. At least for a little bit." I struggle to keep my composure. "Well, for a while now, I guess. My mom's gonna let me know when it's okay to come back, like I told you. My issue is just a family thing."

Just a family thing.

I've really got this stupid story nailed down, huh? Said it so many times, I almost believe it.

I'm not sure he does, though. Still, after studying my face for a while, he slowly nods. "Dad sounds like a dick."

You don't know the half of it. "Total dick."

"Well …" He considers his tea for a second. "I've got to handle a few errands today. Stuff for the bar. I should be back in a few hours. Are you gonna be okay here on your own for a little bit?"

Wait. He's going to let me stay here? While he's off in town doing things?

"Y-Yeah," I finally manage to say. "I'll be okay."

"I can stick around a little longer, if you want. Or you could come with, but … I figured you'd prefer to stay put for a bit, relax, and just take it easy for a few days."

Cooper must be an intuitive man, or else I'm an opened book. "I can hang here."

"There's food in the kitchen if you get hungry, though I don't think I should be gone that long."

"Okay."

He studies me for a moment longer, then finally takes our empty plates and heads back into the house, leaving me on the porch. I glance over my shoulder through the glass door, watching him as he takes the plates to the sink, then disappears down the hall. After he changes, I watch him leave through the front door. From here, I can hear the soft motor of his car, before it fades into the distance, and then I know I'm alone again.

I settle back in my seat, staring ahead at the beach.

My heart starts to race.

The peace of everything unsettles me for some reason. As if I can't trust the calmness when I'm by myself. Is this what I felt last night when I was trying to fall asleep on the couch after he left me alone?

My foot's bouncing in place again.

I can't just sit here. I have to keep busy.

I'm back in the house with his mug of half-drank tea and my empty juice glass. I go to the sink to find our plates there where he brought them, unclean. A glass sits on the counter, too, right by a small saucer full of crumbs.

The silence of the empty house pierces me.

The next minute, the faucet's running as I scrub the plates, then set them in the dish drainer. Glasses, too. Then the saucer. Soon, that activity turns into me scrubbing the countertop itself, then the faucet, and then all around the sink. I notice a smudge on the side of the fridge, which the wet washcloth only succeeds in smearing. My curiosity has me peeking in the cabinets under the sink. Suddenly, I have gloves on, a sponge in hand, and a spray bottle of lemon-scented cleaning fluid with its label torn off.

That's when the madness begins.

Everything in the house is suddenly an unfinished task. Every surface, from the coffee table, to the windows, to the sliding glass door, to the TV screen, to the lampshades, is subjected to my crazed cleaning frenzy. I pull off the sheets from the couch, since I sure as hell won't be sleeping out here, and neatly fold them up. Some kind of frantic music plays in my head as I undo the couch-bed, turning it back into a couch, then get to work cleaning and organizing every damned thing in sight.

I can't stop moving.

Something has taken me over.

I even make Cooper's bed. Then I dust off his desk and adjust the curtains next to them. I pick up some clothes he left by the closet, grab a laundry basket, and start gathering anything I can find, from my old clothes to the towels we used for our showers last night.

This process probably lasts for hours. But it goes by in a blink.

By the time Cooper returns, I'm in the kitchen pulling a couple of clean plates from the cupboard. I glance over my shoulder to find him stopped by the door, startled at what he sees. "Hey there, Coop," I greet him, as if this is something totally normal that he comes home to every day. "Want some lunch? Found your bread and lunchmeat in the fridge. Figured you could go for a sandwich or two."

His eyes scan the rest of the room, taking it in. "Uh ..."

"Go ahead, kick off your shoes, relax. I'll bring you a sandwich. Or do you want two?"

"Did you clean my house?"

I continue assembling the sandwiches and shrug. "Got a little bored, I guess."

"A little bored ...?" He comes into the living room like he doesn't recognize anything. "My TV is ... shiny."

"You get all your errands done?" I ask, going for small talk. What else can I do? I can't stop moving my hands. "I wasn't sure where you do your laundry, since I guess you don't have a washer or dryer, so I just put everything into a basket I left at the end of the hall."

He seems to have spotted it. He doesn't move.

"You're doing a terrible job of relaxing after a day running errands," I point out.

After a moment of overcoming his shellshock, he turns to me. "You didn't have to clean the place."

"I just wanted to," I say, then smile.

And in my smile, I hope he doesn't see my desperation to please him.

I hope he doesn't see the separation anxiety that has all of my nerves feeling instant relief the moment he returned.

I hope these extreme feelings of mine don't scare him away—the one good man I've encountered on my journey.

I present the sandwiches on plates, then shrug. "Wanna eat on the porch, or on the couch?"

Cooper gazes at me. "Let's, uh … take lunch out to the beach. Don't want to drop a single *crumb* in this house you just cleaned."

That's how the pair of us end up on a blanket on the sand, eating sandwiches and watching the waves creep in. Unlike the crowded tourist beach, I feel like I have room out here to stretch and be myself, which is more than I've been able to do for months.

Even if all of the cute houses that line the beach seem to have eyes.

Watching me—the outsider, the stranger, the visitor.

I hope those house-eyes warm up to me, because I have no intention of going anywhere soon—until Coop himself kicks me out.

Once lunch is over, he leans back, propping himself up by his elbows and crossing his legs at the ankle, soaking in the sun. I don't know if it's intentional, but it pulls my eyes straight to his body, where I drink him in from head to toe.

His shirt is barely pulled up at the waist, showing a hint of skin. The shorts he wears seem loose, too, as if just one fast thrust can pull them straight off. It's that little bit of teasing, whether intentional or not, that causes me to instantly wonder what he's got down there.

And suddenly it's all I'm thinking about.

"So I was thinking ..." says Cooper.

I roll onto my side and bring my lips to the little peek-a-boo of his abs showing, kissing him there.

"Whoa, what's going on?" he protests.

My hand goes to the waistband of his shorts, which I let loose the button of. They open for me immediately, like there's a beast down there practically begging to be freed. I tug down his shorts just enough to reveal it.

Holy mother of God, he's big.

His body tenses. "Seany, what're you—?"

I bring my lips to his cock at once. I don't hesitate. I don't ask for permission. I don't build up to anything. I just want to make him feel as good as I feel—and I want him to feel that way *right now.*

"Seany—" he protests again.

Until my lips wrap around the head of his cock, and he shuts right up.

I have no prayer in hell of swallowing the whole length of him, so I focus on the head and first inch or two, using my tongue to tease his dick. He wasn't hard a second ago, but that's quickly changing as he swells and comes to life in my mouth.

The next thing I know, he sits up and has a hand on my shoulder, as if to push me away. "What're you doing?"

I hold his dick with one hand as I lift my face up to give him a look. "I'm doing what I want."

"Out here in front of all of my neighbors?"

"So?"

He tries, with an adorably gentle effort, to release me and my mouth from his hard dick. I go right back down on him in defiance, taking two more inches into my mouth— or should I say throat? For a glorious instant, he can't fight me. I think the man, in fact, lets out a moan and a sigh.

Then sense comes right back to him. "You don't have to do this. I'm not ... I don't expect ... *ungh* ..."

"Having trouble speaking?" I ask when I come off of his dick for a moment. "Maybe you shouldn't try. Just kick back and enjoy."

"I don't want you feeling—*mmph*—" I just swallowed his dick again, this time with more force. "—like you owe me for anything, or like—*Jesus, Mary, and Joseph*—"

I stop for a second. "That's not what this is."

He stares down at me. "Then why—?"

"I want to. I like you."

He seems speechless, his lips left hanging as he stares at my face, bewildered.

"Lean back," I tell him, "let your neighbors get jealous, and just enjoy your post-sandwich mint, alright?"

My mouth wraps around him again, and this time, he doesn't put up a fight. I make love to his dick like I have never made love to anything. It feels so good to hear his breath quicken, to feel his body tense beneath me, to know I'm making him as happy as he's made me.

He lays his hand on my back. Just that soft and caring touch encourages me, as I twist my lips and work him up. He replies with his uneven breaths that crash over me like waves off the Gulf.

"S-Seany ..." he growls.

The urgency in his voice tells me he's there.

I trade my mouth for my hand, then lay his dick over my cheek as I jerk him the rest of the way, continuing to tease the underside with my tongue. With a deep whimper, he erupts all over the side of my face, completely at my mercy as I milk every last drop out of him. Then our eyes lock. I can't imagine what my face looks like, but I sure as hell can see his. He looks happy. Stress-free. Thankful. It's his happiness that makes *me* happy. It's the only thing that makes me happy: his happiness. This man ... the goodness in his heart, which inspires me to be better, to do better ...

I have to tell him.

CHAPTER 8

COOPER

DID I JUST ACQUIRE A HOUSEBOY?

It's nighttime. I'm behind the bar throwing together my hundredth vodka tonic for a customer, but my eyes are on the back of the room where Seany's taken it upon himself to clean off unused tables, sweep the floors, and welcome any customers coming in.

Seriously, I'm at a loss for words.

I don't recognize my life today compared to yesterday.

"So that's the thief you ran off yesterday?" asks Mars, who appears out of nowhere.

My words are slow to come. "Yep."

"And now he's employed here?"

"Not really."

"How do you pay him? With your nuts?"

I face her. "Why're you here again? It's not as busy as yesterday. Doesn't your mom need you at the taqueria?"

"Probably, but it's, like, *way* more fun here these past few days. Plus, you pay more. Working for my mom, she's always acting like she can just 'pay me in love'." She rolls her eyes, then nudges me. "Hey, don't change the subject. I asked about this sticky-fingered *child* you just adopted."

"He's not a *child.*"

"I still don't trust him." She squints at him across the room, then shrugs. "But I will admit, he *does* work hard."

"He does," I agree.

"Of course, he *has* to, to pay off all of the peanuts and soda he stole."

"He was just hungry," I point out lightly. "Can't blame the guy for just trying to survive. The world out there is harsh enough. He needs a break, doesn't he?"

Mars gives me a pointed look. "Seems like he stole something else, too."

I lift an eyebrow. "What's that?"

She skirts around the counter to make her rounds, leaving me to wonder. I continue serving customers, now and then glancing at the back of the room, still mystified by the enigma that is the eighteen-year-old-on-the-run whose name I will still firmly believe really is Seany—*and whose story I will remain skeptical about.*

The truth is, I don't know what to think. It's been way too long since I've been intimate with anyone, let alone a kid less than half my age. To have my self-imposed spell of celibacy broken by some intoxicatingly adorable twink that I just met yesterday is something I need time to process. He makes me confused. He makes me unsettled. He makes me sandwiches for lunch.

And he makes my heart flutter like a fucking butterfly.

He makes me feel like I'm floating everywhere I go.

He makes me spill vodka over my hand. "Fuck, sorry," I say to a customer as I force my eyes off of Seany across the room and pay better attention to what I'm doing.

I wish I had someone I could talk to about this.

For knowing damned well everyone on the island, my list of true confidants is pretty damned short and sad.

Sometime later, I notice one of the lights hanging over the front steps outside has gone out, so instead of troubling Chase or Seany, I handle it myself. When the rush has died down enough to leave the front to Chase, I head out to the front steps with a stepladder and a bulb in hand.

It's while screwing that bulb that I spot someone across the way, near the beach.

The sight of him causes my hand to freeze mid-screw.

I don't believe my eyes. *Is that—?*

81

Noisy half-dressed men walk up the steps to enter the bar, for a moment blocking my view entirely, and by the time they've made their way inside, I've lost sight of the guy near the beach …

The guy I recognized … *or thought I recognized.*

Maybe it wasn't him at all.

Of course it wasn't him. How could it be? It's been ten years since I've seen him. He would be twenty-eight now. I doubt I'd even recognize him so easily.

The guy who broke my heart into three pieces.

One piece he took for sport. The second he pitched into the Gulf of Mexico like garbage. The third, smallest piece, that's what I have left, the part that still beats in my chest.

The only part I have left to give anyone.

It wasn't him, I decide, certain of it. It's astonishing what my experience with Seany is resurrecting inside me. Feelings I thought I'd never know again. Fears, joys, and anxieties I was certain I'd never feel at my age. I assumed all the doors were closed—and Seany came and kicked all of them wide open.

Maybe that's what unsettles me the most.

After the bulb's changed, I rush inside, cut through the crowd, and step into the inventory closet. Once the door is shut behind me, I tap a name and put the phone to my ear.

"Need my help at the bar again?" asks my pal Adrian the moment he answers. "Not sure if I can get away to help you tonight. We've got a birthday party and six—yeah, you heard me right—*six* anniversaries. I think one of them is gonna pop the question. Fuck me, you'd think Thalassa was some romantic restaurant by the beach or something."

"The kid is staying at my place."

He pauses. "Wait. Who?"

"The kid from last night. It's the reason I ran off. He's who I ran after, the kid I asked you about."

"That underage twink you were describing last night?"

"He's eighteen. And he's in a bad place in his life right now. I don't know all the details, but … I just felt the need to help him out. All the hotels were booked, couldn't hook him up with anything, so I brought him home."

"Like a lost puppy. Adorable. And I thought hanging at the Hopewell's last night was fun. Finn and his boyfriend kept asking about you, by the way."

"The kid's here at the bar now helping out. He's acting like I've hired him."

"Ooh, a level three clinger, huh? Is that the problem? That why you called? Need to shake him loose?"

"No, no. I'm just …" I lean against the wall with such a heavy sigh, it could blow down a door. "I'm just worried whether I'm doing the right thing is all."

"Of course you are. Everyone knows how you like to take care of those sweet boys in need. It's kinda your thing. Isn't that the reason everyone calls you Daddy Coop?"

"I don't want the boy to get the wrong idea, like I'm taking advantage of his situation."

"So ... what you're saying is, you two *didn't* have sex last night?"

"No, we didn't." I hesitate. "But he did blow me on the beach this afternoon out in bright daylight."

"What??"

"Shut up, Adrian."

"Who are you?? When did you get this exciting??"

I throw my head back with a sigh. "You've probably had a dozen far more salacious things happen to you every weekend before you met what's-his-name, but—"

"You forgot the love of my life's name?"

"—this is a pretty big deal to me. I don't hook up with cute, young guys. His staying with me is just supposed to be a quick thing until he gets back on his feet, that's it."

"Sorry, but ... I don't think it's just some quick thing you've got on your hands, Coop."

I shake my head. "Maybe I'm overthinking this."

"Maybe he needs more than just a roof over his head."

I consider that for a moment. I think about the sweet, needy look in Seany's eyes earlier today. Our time on the beach. His insistence to clean up my house. To make lunch for us. To show how useful and loving he can be.

Is something else happening here?

Something right under my nose?

"Gotta go," Adrian says suddenly. "Stepped away for too long. You'd better reconsider coming to the big bonfire Monday night. Bring your new friend! Maybe he'll become one of us. Wouldn't be the worst idea. Later, man."

He hangs up, leaving me listening to the muffled noise of the bar on the other side of the door and pulling on the strings of my tangled ball of thoughts.

What if Adrian is right? *What if Seany needs more than just a roof over his head?*

The question follows me home several hours later as I drive back in my car with Seany. "I took you for more of a pickup kind of guy," he murmurs, picking at something on his shirt, which I lent him for tonight.

"A pickup kind of guy?"

"As opposed to a car. I think I got something on your shirt." He keeps picking at it. "Sorry."

"Just toss it in the basket when we're back." After we come to a stop at an intersection, I glance at him, gnawing on my lip. "So ... did you try calling your family again?"

His face changes. Then he stares ahead blankly, as if I just told him a ghost was sitting on the hood of the car.

I nod with understanding. "No worries. Just curious."

His blank stare continues the rest of the way home. We park by the curb in front of my house, and he still seems to be in a daze. Should I not have asked anything?

We're halfway to the front door when: "Coop?"

I stop and turn. "Yeah?"

"I … I just wanted to say …" Seany is staring down at my chest, like he's ashamed to look me in the eye. "I need to tell you something. Confess something."

I try not to assume the worst. "Alright. What is it?"

He folds his arms over his chest as tightly as he can. "The thing is … I won't be getting any 'okay' from home." He closes his eyes. "I lied. My mom left when I was nine. My dad hates me. He doesn't want me back. He probably doesn't care if I'm alive or dead. He's an abusive asshole. I should have left with my mom somehow, but I was scared, and she was a pill-popping coward. I … couldn't stay there another day. I couldn't stay there another second. I wasn't even able to finish my senior year. I … I-I had to go." His voice shakes. "I don't have a …" He fights back tears. "I-I don't have a home anymore. At all."

It breaks my heart, hearing him say all of this.

Yet somehow, I think I already knew.

"I understand if you—" He almost chokes. "—if this is all too much for you, more than you'd bargained for. I'm sure the last damned thing you want is s-some *problem* like me sitting on your doorstep. I just—I don't have anywhere to go. I-I can leave if you want me to. I'll understand. I'm sorry I lied. I'm sorry I—"

He flinches when I come up and bring my arms around him, hugging him to my chest.

He grows still, seeming unsure what to do.

I stroke the back of his hair. "You're okay, Seany."

"I ... I just ..."

"You're safe here." I bring my hand to his back, which I gently start to rub. "You don't have to leave. Not until you're ready. Not until you want to. Not until—"

"Really?"

"Really."

He swallows. "And ... what if I never want to leave?"

I don't know what his fate is. Whether I'm a stepping stone on his path to finding himself, or I'm the safe nest he finally discovers a home in. Regardless, the outcome is the same: I'll have helped him find his place.

"Then so be it," I reply, still rubbing his back. "Stay."

CHAPTER 9

COOPER

SEANY CLENCHES ME TIGHTER.

The silence of the warm night air wraps around us, filled only by our deep breaths as we stand in front of my house. Not even a car appears to disturb the peace we've found in each other's arms.

He stirs in my arms. "Can I sleep with you again?"

I glance over his shoulder at my dark, unlit house.

This afternoon's time on the beach flashes before my eyes. The sun. The sand. The feel of his body against mine. His mouth engulfing me. The look of curiosity in his eyes. His determination to make me happy.

Why do I get the sense he wants to take care of me as much as I want to take care of him?

Every single one of my expectations of who Seany is has been shattered.

Could this really work between us? Whatever it is?

Whatever it's becoming?

In another hour, the pair of us lie on my bed, cuddled together just as we were the night before. This time, Seany is facing me, nuzzled into my chest with my arms wrapped around him like a blanket, safe and snug. Now and then, he shifts and squirms in my hold, as if trying to press his body more tightly against mine. I respond by tightening my hold on him, holding him close. I'm in a tank top and a pair of clingy boxer-briefs. He's in just a pair of gray boxer-briefs himself, insisting he's more comfortable in his underwear. The ceiling fan is on a low setting, sending waves of cool air over our bodies as we lie here in the semidarkness, just a slit of porch light coming in from the window.

"I know it's just the second night," he says, his voice soft and quiet, "but I love being in your arms."

I smile against his hair. "I'm glad to hear it."

"But I feel happy with you, too. I feel like I finally met someone who genuinely cares about me. I …" He lets out a soft sigh. "I like you, Cooper."

I slide a hand up and down the smooth, soft skin of his back, gentle and soothing. "I like you, too."

"I mean ... *really* like you."

My hand stops. "Seany ..."

"Please don't tell me I'm just a kid or don't know what I'm talking about. I know what feelings are."

"Okay, but—"

"I'm not confused. I know you're a good man. I know you truly care about me. And I know ..." He tightens up. "I know this is a lot. Sorry. I've always been like this."

"Like what?"

"Intense. Coming on too strong. But ..." He lifts his head from my chest to get a look at my face. "But when I know it's the real thing, I've gotta be bold. My time on the streets has taught me to know what you have and to hold on to it tightly, or else it slips away. I ... I can't let you just think I'm here freeloading off of you. You deserve to be happy, too. We fulfill all of each other's needs, don't we? We could be good for each other, Coop."

I shut my eyes.

It isn't a lie. That gaping hole in my life, that hole I fill with my bar, with my porch plants, with my hobbies ... it's been a lot less empty these past couple of days.

Past couple of days ...? Am I hearing myself? "You are young. I know you don't want me to say it, but it's the truth. There are tons of guys your age on this island, guys you'd be happier to spend time with, to form relationships with, and maybe to fall in love with someday."

"Coop, I don't want some fickle *boy* my age. I want a man like you. Someone who knows the world, who can protect me from it, but also experience it with me. I want someone I can take care of, too, as much as he takes care of me. It's obvious. We're good for each other."

He's really selling the dream. If I just play along with him and forget everything I know, I can believe the pair of us could make this work. "You've known me for less than two days," I remind him.

"But does it feel like two days?" He searches my eyes. To him, it's anything but a joke. "It wasn't a coincidence I ended up at your bar. You caught me. You've been looking for a guy like me, a guy who fits right into your life. Our relationship began with you literally *looking* for me."

I can't convince him that what he's seeing is a fantasy. It would be cruel to suggest that, considering the happy, pleading look in his eyes. Who am I to shatter that dream?

I know better. He will wake up one of these days and realize his life is still awaiting him out there, with another guy, with another dream-filled young man, with someone who can give him more of a future.

I smile. "You're adorable."

"Don't patronize me."

"Just another fact. You are. You're adorable. Who in their right mind would take a look at you and not just …?"

He stares at me, waiting for the rest of that sentence.

Fall in love?

Was that what I was about to say?

He must assume that's exactly what I was going to say, because he brings his lips to mine. I realize I can't resist him. Our kissing intensifies. Then his hands reach around my body and start grappling with my tank, desperate to get it out of the way. I respond the only way I can, by kissing him right back, by holding him against me like a delicate treasure, all mine, someone I know I may only be able to cherish for a moment.

His hand slips down between our bodies, and I feel his fingers delicately slide over the smooth, silky material of my boxer-briefs.

Prickles of delight rocket through my body. The touch is so sensitive, it feels like I'm wearing nothing at all when his fingertips graze over my crotch.

"Seany, baby ..." I start.

"Yes," he says, misunderstanding, "I want to be your baby. I want to be yours. All yours."

For all of my sense, I suddenly have none. I fall right into the dream he just painted for us and give in, kissing him deeply. His hand massages and kneads my crotch with such strength, I can't help but feel the hunger for him rage through my body. My hands are out of my control as I take hold of his body, then slide them down his back to cup his tight little ass. It's been too long. I miss this. I *need* this.

I flip him onto his back, then drag my mouth down his body. His nipples become my two favorite candies as I lick them like lollipops, one at a time. The noise of Seany as he squirms beneath me only encourages me more. I wrap my lips around one and suck until he cries out unintelligibly, unable to contain himself. His body is like a buffet of sexy, delicious snacks I can't get enough of. His skin, smooth and supple. His abs, firm and pliable. And as I reach the waistband of his underwear, they peel downward so easily, it's like they're inviting me inside with no reservation.

His dick is so hard, it pops right out and flexes against the side of my face, desperate to be pleasured. I have never seen a cock more aesthetically beautiful than his. The skin is soft to the touch, even when hard, and not too veiny. I open my mouth to the cockhead, and it slips right in, like it's returning to a home it's never been in. Seany sighs with relief and surprise as I suck on just the head, which I know will drive him wild. My tongue teases the underside, tickling it, titillating it, until I know there's surely no way he could possibly get harder and more ready than he is.

Then I take hold of his hips and swallow his cock.

Seany buckles beneath me, groaning his happiness.

I wonder if he's ever known pleasure like this before. Am I the first one in his life to suck him off who actually knows what he's doing?

I lift from his cock to get a look at his face. He is in a

complete state of bliss. He lifts his head from the pillow to meet my eyes. I feel like we're connected beyond words and pretty speeches. We get each other in a way no one has to understand or explain.

He needs something I can give him.

I need something back.

And he's more than willing to give.

"Can I make love to you?"

I lift an eyebrow in surprise.

"I want it so, so badly," he whimpers. "I want to feel myself inside of you. Please."

I don't know if he realizes what he's asking.

I've only bottomed once before, and I said I wouldn't do it again. It wasn't my thing.

"I've done it before," he goes on. "Seriously. I know what I'm doing. I won't suck at it."

I love his eagerness to prove himself.

His determination.

That hungry, needy look in Seany's eyes is something I am finding it harder and harder to say no to.

I'm going to spoil him rotten, aren't I?

"I'll allow it this one time," I tell him. "But I—"

"I'll stop if you tell me to stop," he insists eagerly. "I won't hurt you, I promise."

"Hurt me?" I snort. "You can't hurt me, boy. I can take it. I just want you to understand why I'm allowing you to do this. I'm allowing it this one time because I *trust* you."

His eyes turn big. "I appreciate that."

"Good. Are you ready to be inside me?"

"Yes. Please, yes."

I reach for my nightstand and pull out the essentials. As I straddle his legs, I roll a condom over his cock, which seems to succeed in making him even harder. Then I open the lube, squeeze some out, and tease it down his length. Seany bites his lip and moans as I stroke the lube up and down his cock to slick it up. His hands find purchase on my hips, stroking my sides with anticipation as I prep him. I watch him the whole time, feeling a strange excitement as I observe each of his eager, happy facial expressions.

There is something so deeply satisfying about giving him this experience, I can't put it into words.

After taking off my underwear to lube my hole, he sits up suddenly. "Can I do it?"

I show my surprise, then chuckle. "Really?"

"Yes. I want to do it. Please."

He really wants the whole damned experience, doesn't he? "Alright."

I give him the lube. He squeezes some onto his fingers, then reaches around me with this adorably wicked look on his face. When he starts teasing my hole with his soft, slick fingers, my jaw drops. I wasn't expecting it to feel so good. It's a ticklish sort of happy electricity that chases its way up and down my body. I never thought my hole could feel this sensitive again.

Okay, alright, this is about a million times better than lubing myself up.

He's teased my hole into such a relaxed state, I feel his fingers start to slip in. I moan and rock my eyes back. He removes his fingers, takes hold of me by my hips, then guides his hard, yearning cock to my hole.

I meet his eyes. "Are you ready to be inside me?"

Seany bites his lip, then nods eagerly.

I slowly start to lower myself down on him, and after a moment of soft pressure, I feel his cockhead go in.

I can't testify as to how my face looks right now, but I did not expect the simple act of him entering me to feel this insanely amazing. My jaw drops. I lurch forward. And I am captured all over again by the determined look on his face. He grits his teeth as he smiles, nose wrinkled up, as he lets himself slide in and out of me, just a little at first, then deeper and deeper. Our faces are near one another's as we lock our gazes like horns. He is the perfect size and shape to slide in and out of me with little resistance, and with each thrust, I feel my insides come undone more and more.

When I feel his lubed fingers wrap around my hard cock, which bounces between us, it catches me by pleasant surprise. "*Thank you, Coop,*" he whispers against my face as he starts stroking me.

He picks up the pace, both with his thrusts and with stroking my cock. I take over stroking my cock as he grabs me by the hips, then take hold of his lips with my own. Our breaths come and go like shattering ocean waves as we get closer and closer together.

He unlocks our kiss to whimper, "I'm close."

"*Me too*," I hiss right back.

When we fall over the edge together, I feel every ounce of my tension release at once. His moans turn into grunts as he empties himself inside me. I cling to him tighter as I let loose between our bodies, wave after wave, spilling all over his chest as well as my own.

Our lips find each other's in the blissful madness.

The aggression of our orgasms turns soft, fading away to our gentle kissing as we embrace the moment, coming down from our peaks.

"*Fuck, that was amazing ...*" I whisper, so overcome by the height I just reached, I'm nearly laughing.

He grins against my face. "*I've never felt better, Coop. I'm so happy I'm here. I'm so fucking happy.*"

Then we say the rest with our tender kisses, his cock still inside me, mine resting on his abs. I realize suddenly neither one of us wants to let go. If only kisses could last forever. If only moments like these weren't so precious and perfect that the mere idea of them ending is terrifying.

Maybe it doesn't have to end.

Maybe the terror is just an illusion.

"I know what I want to do next," I tell him.

It's like he's coming out of a dream when he replies. "What's next? Braiding each other's hair?"

I take hold of his hand. "Come with me."

A moment later, the pair of us are stripped and in the shower. The water runs over us as we cuddle in the narrow stall, blanketed in steam, his back against my chest. I run the bar of soap gently over his body, cleaning every inch of his skin. With his cute butt bumping and grinding against my cock in the shower, it's a challenge not to think about talking him into round two already—with *me* on top.

But then I pull out the shampoo, and as I start to lather it up in his hair, something else takes over me. That need to take care of him, to nurture him, to love on him in the way he really needs.

Here in this shower, washing with Seany, it's the first time in a long time I realize I don't feel that empty hole in me anymore. I need this just as much as I hope he needs me. This is what I've wanted all along. This, right here.

Us. *Him.*

As we caress in bed an hour later, fresh and clean, I hold him close as I stroke his hair. He falls asleep first, and I realize as I lie there listening to him breathe that he trusts me with all his heart. He feels safe with me. He's happy.

He's home.

CHAPTER 10

SEANY

THIS TIME, *I'M* MAKING BREAKFAST.

Pancakes, to be precise. It's the only thing I know how to make that would impress Cooper enough. I'm the first one up, so I get right to work in the kitchen while he sleeps in. When he comes down the hall, wiping sleep out of his eyes and yawning, he blinks with surprise as he finds me at the counter, humming, and cooking up pancakes.

He might also be reacting to the fact that I found an apron in the closet, which I swiftly put on before getting to work on breakfast.

And other than the skimpy apron, I'm kinda naked.

I give him a coy glance over my shoulder. "Morning. Ready for the best pancakes you've ever had?"

He grins. "Well, damn, if this is any indication of what my Sunday is about to be like ..."

I give him a wink. "Take a seat. Pancakes will be ready soon."

He's about to learn this is more than just an indication of his day.

I want to make every moment amazing.

After filling our bellies with pancakes, the rest of the morning is spent lounging together on the couch, with the TV on, the breeze seeping in through the windows making the curtains dance, as we share random stories with each other about our lives. All of our walls are down. Nothing is off limits. I even tell him about the fact that I wet the bed until I was thirteen—a mortifying fact—and he admitted to me that someone pantsed him at a school dance freshman year and the whole school saw his junk.

We crack each other up.

We grow close with every secret shared.

Then we kiss and get lost in each other's lips for too long and forget whatever it is we were planning to do.

Is this how every day of our lives together could be?

He introduces me to each plant he keeps on his back porch, which I noticed, but never asked about. He teaches me what he does to care for each one every day, and as he shares nerdy little factoids about them, I realize there's a reason he's telling me this at all.

He expects me to stick around.

Good, because I have no plans to leave.

When he goes out to take care of his errands, I go right along with him. He doesn't seem to mind. In fact, he smiles the whole time he drives around town, whistling along to whatever song's on the radio. Was he always this capable of acting free and happy? I hang my head from the window and let the breeze toss around my messy hair.

One errand has us stopping by the arcade, where he has something to discuss with the owner. I stand around his car outside, basking in the sunlight as I wait for him.

The arcade doors pop open, and out comes a familiar face, but it isn't Cooper's.

He comes to a stop, recognizing me.

I stare back at him, and all of my peace is broken.

"Hey, I know you," he says.

Fear fills my bones. It's the guy I sat next to on the beach just a few days ago—the guy whose thirty bucks still sits in my pocket, untouched.

I see my whole future crumble before my eyes.

My life here. My happiness with Cooper. My paradise.

Then the guy smiles. "You're from the beach, right? A few days ago? I think your name was Clyde …?"

Oh. I forgot I gave him that name.

"What's wrong?" He comes right up to me. "You look like you're freaked out or something."

Is he not mad? *Or did he not realize ...?* "I'm just ... I was just waiting on someone."

"Someone? Oh. There aren't many people inside, other than Cooper talking to Michael about business stuff. Did you forget my name already?" he teases me. "I'm Toby."

I try to smile, but honestly, I'm still panicked. "Nice to meet you, Toby. Well, *again*, I mean."

He smiles. "Well, I won't keep you. I was just blowing off some steam on the games, like I do every weekend. Got to get back home. Boyfriend's working on something. We should maybe hang out sometime, since you're new here, too. Wait, didn't we establish that?" Toby seems to confuse himself suddenly. "Or am I assuming you're new here?"

Is this when I make a real commitment?

Is this when I decide I'm definitely staying?

Can I really stay in a place where my conscience isn't clear? "I, uh ... have to confess something."

Toby lifts an eyebrow. "Confess something? Oh. Are *you* the guy who has the new Mortal Kombat high score competing with mine?"

If only it was something that innocent. "No. I, uh ..."

"Yeah?"

Suddenly I can't say it. So instead, I just fish the thirty bucks out of my pocket and extend it to him. He squints at the wadded up bit of cash before letting me slap it into his palm. He inspects it with uncertainty. "I ... I don't get it. Do you owe me for something? Or—?"

"I took it from you." My heart hammers in my chest. "I took it when you went down to get in the water. You left all your things there on the beach, and I ..." *I can barely breathe*. "I'm sorry, Toby."

He seems to work it out in his head. Then it clicks. "Oh. Y'know, I ... I honestly just thought I'd spent it at the antiques store on the boardwalk. My boyfriend thought I'd gotten art supplies, and then I was confused, and ..." Then he meets my eyes. "You stole this from me?"

My insides are shaking. My *teeth* are shaking. I'm not even sure I've taken one breath since I uttered the words. "Y-Yes," I manage.

Toby studies the cash for a moment longer, then lifts his eyes to mine. "I should probably be upset or something. But ever since moving here, I've realized I need to forgive and be more understanding. Why should I be angry about it when you're here trying to make good on something bad?" He smiles. "That's something that should be appreciated. Good for you, Clyde. You did the right thing."

I stare at him, stunned.

Is he serious?

"In fact," he goes on, then takes my hand and presses the cash right back into my palm, "you obviously took it for a reason, and I'm suspecting you need it more. So how about you keep that, alright? And I *still* insist we should hang out sometime."

He's crazy. He has to be. Who does this?

"The name is Seany," I say rather suddenly.

Now *that* makes Toby gasp. "Wait. And you lied about your name?? I take it all back! I only wanted to be friends when I thought you were named after one of the Pac-Man ghosts! Just kidding," he quickly adds with a silly laugh. "I like it. Nice to meet you! My name really is Toby, though."

"Thank you, Toby." I fidget with the thirty bucks still in my hand. It feels odd, accepting it back. Is everyone on this island so fucking forgiving?

"So how does it feel now?"

I don't follow. "How does what feel?"

"This place. Your 'paradise' you were looking for after leaving San Antonio. Is it better than a few days ago?"

This boy really remembers everything. I glance at the arcade, thinking of Cooper. Our morning. Last night. All of our laughter. The racing of my heart. Thinking of it all, a smile softly touches my lips. "I think it's ... a lot closer to paradise now."

"I'm glad to hear it, Seany. Phew, I've gotta go now. There's a ton of Pride things going on all week, including a thing here at the arcade, street food vendors, an art show ... all down Cassanova Street, every night this week."

"Pride things?"

"Yeah! The Hopewell Fair does stuff on the weekends, but the weekdays also have a lot going on. Is that not your thing? Vann has a booth at the north end of Cassanova Street. I hope we get visitors. It'll be fun! You can hang out at our booth for a while if you want. Check out some of the other cool things happening. Stuff yourself with tasty street food. Oh, oops, now I'm *really* late. Gotta go."

I watch Toby make his hurried way down the road and around the corner on foot. Still emotionally bewildered, I barely notice Cooper coming out of the arcade a second later. He comes up to me with a smile. "You alright?"

The forgiveness Toby just showed me has me feeling dazed. "I think I just made a new friend."

"Oh? Who's that?"

"A chipper, overly forgiving guy named Toby."

"Ah, yes. Moved here recently with his boyfriend from Spruce. Always at the arcade. Seems like a nice guy."

"He wants me to hang out with him tomorrow night."

Coop's face changes. "Hmm. At the bonfire? Haven't been to one of those in ages."

Bonfire? "Not sure. He was talking about street food and art and Pride stuff."

"Oh, that. There's stuff going on all around town, yeah. I forgot about all the street fair stuff on Cassanova."

"You said there's a bonfire also?"

He shrugs that off. "They're lame. Same boring crowd hanging around a fire complaining about tourists."

It sounds kinda fun, too. But I just chuckle and give a careless shrug. "Yeah. It sounds ... super lame."

He studies me for a second. "You want to walk around the street fair tomorrow night? Meet up with your friend?"

"I ..." Am I being tested? Is this a test or something? Suddenly everything feels weird. "Nah. They're ... He's ... not really my friend or anything. I only just met him."

"You sure?"

I give one last glance at the corner where Toby hurried off, then nod. "Yeah, I'm sure. Let's get outta here."

When evening rolls around, I'm with Coop at the Easy Breezy. He doesn't mention the street fair or bonfire again, and neither do I. Any weirdness I felt before is forgotten as I step in to bus tables, walk the floor, and greet customers. To my surprise, I'm totally at ease like I've been working this job for years. I bet even the guests just assume I'm one of the locals, doing my usual weekend gig.

Maybe it's another skill I've picked up along the way.

Just slipping right in wherever I am.

Even the cold-shouldered girl named Mars warms up to me—but only after giving me an ultimate shakedown: "If you hurt Coop, I hurt you, that's it, that's the only rule. Got it?" I give a nervous nod, and then she becomes instant smiles. "You and I are gonna be best friends, Seany."

As the evening goes on, I feel the weekend drawing to a close. Some people have gone home already, needing to be back before work on Monday. Others linger around here and there, sucking up every last second of their vacation in Dreamwood. There are several more who plan to stay the week here for all the extra Pride festivities.

It's a really special, warm feeling, to know I don't have to leave come the final hour of the day when the island at last begins to settle, like the smoke after a fireworks show.

Cooper and I take off, leaving the closing shift up to his trusty bartender Chase. The pair of us sit on the bottom step of the Easy Breezy, gazing out at the nearly emptied beach and the lingering light in the sky.

I'm squeezed next to Cooper, like he's the only thing in the world that keeps me warm. I turn to him. "What're you thinking about?"

His eyes are full of dreams as he gazes off. "Nothing."

"Hey, don't hold back now. Aren't we supposed to be telling each other everything?"

He snorts, then glances at me. "Alright. You want the truth? I was just thinking about the corniest thing in the world. My little fleeting dream."

I lift an eyebrow. "Fleeting dream …?"

He points off toward the Quicksilver Strand. "See the boardwalk? I sit out here sometimes when the bar's slow, and there are always couples walking by on it. Older men who've been together forever … or sweet young lovers holding hands, stars in their eyes …"

"You wished you were one of them?"

"I'd never admit it out loud, but …" He chuckles. "I guess so. Yes. That's my fleeting dream."

I slide my hand into his, weaving our fingers together. It draws him from his thoughts and brings him right to me, where he meets my eyes.

I smirk. "Not so much a dream anymore, huh?"

Cooper gazes at me with curiosity.

Of course that's how we end the night: two lost souls, far from lost anymore, walking along the boardwalk with the water crashing below our feet. Hand-in-hand, we stroll along the planks of creaking wood as the sun sets beyond the water, with the bright and glittering storefronts of the Quicksilver Strand at our backs. It feels like a dream.

This place is really living up to its name.

When we stop by the banister to share a kiss, I realize I'm standing in a paradise where all of my troubles are so far away, I wonder if I ever had them in the first place. Paradise isn't just for the deep-pocketed or deserving. It's wherever you find it. In a kiss shared on a boardwalk. In the cool waves lapping at your feet. In the breeze caught in your hair. In a place called Dreamwood Isle, a paradise set aside just for me and Cooper.

A place where my life can finally begin.

CHAPTER 11

COOPER

I STARE AT SEANY FROM THE DESK, CONFLICTED.

He looks so peaceful sleeping on my bed, cuddling a body-length pillow I think he believes is me. I wonder when was the last time he had a weekend like this—safe, fed, happy.

I should be feeling good. I should be happy, too.

But then I think about him hanging out with Toby. And Vann. And other boys his age, who are all over the island. I think about what a happy and fulfilled life for Seany could really look like, if he'd just see it himself.

But does that happy life still include me?

Is he just using me to feel better about life again?

Or am I using him to fill the voids in my own?

It's only been one weekend. I know how young hearts wander. He thinks he's happy now. He thinks he's won the lottery with a man like me.

But he will get used to this, no matter how much he insists he won't. He will start to notice other men. His eyes will catch other eyes. He will start to wonder.

My house will start to feel like a cage.

I will go from being his daddy to being his *dad*.

He doesn't know this yet. He's still floating high up in the clouds. But I've seen enough, I've lived long enough, and I know human nature.

I couldn't help but think about this all night, watching him working the Easy Breezy, getting along with both the locals and vacationers, making his job look like a breeze, pun intended. He didn't notice, but I kept staring at him as I worked the bar, torturing myself with thoughts.

Long-term thoughts.

Realistic thoughts.

Feet-on-the-ground thoughts.

Is it foolish to expect this to actually last between us?

I should enjoy whatever this is for as long as it dares to last—and fight my own human nature to selfishly keep the boy all to myself. Seany deserves someone who will truly keep his best interest in mind, not just another leeching demon who will use him for his pretty face.

No matter how tempting it might be to do just that in my weakest moment.

Like when he talked me into bottoming for him, and I was nothing but clay in his hands.

Like earlier this evening, when the pair of us walked hand-in-hand on the boardwalk, at last fulfilling one of my lifetime fantasies.

Like right now, listening to him sleep, and feeling my heart crushing inward with hope.

Hope is deadly.

I head outside through the back door, step out onto the porch, and listen to the waves crash. Only the pale starlight provides evidence of their existence as I drift away with the rolling waves, my mind afloat on an imaginary raft, hoping an answer comes.

But it isn't an answer that comes. "Can't sleep?"

I turn to find Seany standing at the sliding glass door, in only another pair of boxer-briefs I gave him, which hide nothing. It seems to be the last thing on his mind as he studies me with concern, his pretty eyes glistening in the porch light.

"Nothing you need to worry about. It's common."

"Common? You're an insomniac?"

"My mind never shuts off." I turn back to the waves crashing in the semidarkness. "Go back to bed, Seany."

He comes up to the banister instead. "Something is weird with you. I can tell. I know you."

I'm compelled to laugh at that. "You know me? Seany, you've known me for the better part of a weekend."

"I can know a person after one hour."

"That so?"

"I know whether they're good or bad."

"So you're Santa Claus now?"

"It's a special talent you learn from the streets." Seany hops onto the banister next to me with ease, swinging a leg over to straddle the railing. "I've learned a lot of useful shit from the streets."

I glance at the side of his face, watching him stare off at the distant waves. Is this still part of the armor he wears? Puffing himself up? Letting nothing and no one faze him? Faking it until he truly does possess the confidence and fearlessness he wants to exude? Or can a person so young really know who someone else is within the space of an hour? Either I'm playing into his game or seeing something he can't because of his reckless, youthful pride.

"Mmm, it smells so nice out here," says Seany, nearly moaning the words.

I smile. "That so?"

"Salty and briny and fresh." He closes his eyes and tilts back his head, letting the breeze play over his face. "I feel like I've barely scraped the surface of what this place has to offer. Every time you think you've seen everything, you see something else."

What I wouldn't give to have his fresh point of view. I remember the sense of wonder I had when I washed up on the shores of this beach town, figuratively speaking. Stars were in my eyes. Possibilities thumped in my heart. Every breath I took was filled with dreams and promise.

"Things are turning around for me," says Seany with a lift of his chin. "The bad days are behind me."

Hope can be deadly, I did say. Even dreams have teeth. It's safe to admire the beauty and splendor of lightning, but only at a distance.

If it strikes close enough, it'll kill you. "How can you be so sure, Seany?"

"I just am. Look at me now. I found Dreamwood. I'm surrounded by dreams. By happiness. By … this delicious, seaside air." He peers at me thoughtfully. "I found you."

"Yes, you did." I take a breath. "And … you can find so much more than me, too."

His face wrinkles. "What do you mean?"

"Dreamwood Isle is full of people, Seany. That's all I mean. Lots of good people … if you know where to look."

"I know. I've been here for a month now. I get the gist. I'm—Wait, what are you getting at?"

He's already onto me. I pivot. "I just mean you … have the potential of finding a real family here."

"Like you?"

"Like … whatever real family means to you. You can find a lot more than just *me* here. You deserve a place like this, a place with possibilities. You've had it rough."

He shrugs. "So? I don't let it get to me."

"I mean, the shit you've probably had to deal with …"

"Hey, Coop?"

I look at him. "Yeah?"

"Do me a favor. Don't pity me."

"Huh?"

"I hear it in your voice. Don't do that. Don't pity me. I don't want anyone's pity."

"I … I don't pity you. I admire you."

"Don't admire me, either. I'm not an angel. I'm not an honorable, war-torn hero. I'm just some unlucky kid who needed to get the fuck away from the battleground that was his former home." He doesn't look at me, casting his words to the sea. "Sorry for saying 'fuck'." He frowns. "And for saying it again just now."

"You don't have to be sorry for words, Seany." I look at him. "Listen, I didn't mean for my admiration to feel … patronizing. I just look at you and … and I see a strong, smart young man who can have the whole world if he wants. A young man with … with a lot of life left to live."

He wrinkles his face. "A lot of life …?"

"Just promise me something, Seany. If you really want

114

to stay here, if you want to show your appreciation for me, other than working your tail off at the Easy Breezy."

He faces me. "Promise what?"

I peer into his sensitive eyes. Even when he ran away from me not a handful of days ago with a handful of salted nuts in his palm and his eyes were hard and defiant, I saw the sensitivity in them then, too. I saw his troubled soul.

No one his age should have such a troubled soul.

They should be free. Open. Explorative. Full of wonder and insatiable curiosity.

I take hold of his hand, startling him. It's to our clasped hands that I say, "Promise me you'll keep your doors open. All of them. Every door you find."

"I … I don't understand."

"You don't have to. My words will make sense when they're meant to make sense."

"Then how can I promise—?"

"Keep your doors open, Seany. You're no one's toy. You're no one's property. You deserve the love and dignity of a prince." I run my thumb over the top of his hand. His fingers are so soft and gentle, it breaks my heart. "Promise me you'll remember that."

He struggles with his thoughts as he gazes at me. I see him wrestling with what to say.

Then: "Okay. I promise. You happy?"

My lips curl up, giving in to a smile just as the breeze

picks up, brushing past my face. "I'll be happy as long as you keep that promise."

Seany frowns in thought, but doesn't protest further.

My hand slips from his as I step away from the banister and turn my back to the waves. "Think I'm ready to sleep now. Need to make sure we're ready for the week, just in case we get extra business from all the Pride stuff going on. Plus my usual Monday morning crap."

"Okay. I'll … I'll stay out here a little longer, if that's alright."

I nod. "Of course."

"Goodnight, Coop."

I consider saying something else, then refrain. "Have a good night yourself, Seany." I head back inside.

It's a mere eleven minutes later while I'm in bed that I hear him slip in through the back door. After a trip to the toilet to pee, he quietly pads into the bedroom, climbs into bed, and snuggles by my side without a word. I adjust, taking him into my arms and being the big spoon. Then we grow still in the dark, our bodies pressed against one another—a perfect, snuggly fit.

Another ten minutes later, my eyes are still open.

My nose, lost in Seany's soft hair, my lips at the back of his sweet, supple neck.

My thoughts are everywhere. My heart, too.

Am I overthinking this? Am I causing a problem when

there isn't one? He already knows he's free to leave. He's well aware I'm not keeping him or claiming him.

He has expressed how happy he is with me.

Why can't I believe it and just roll with it?

Because he's young and doesn't know better, I remind myself. *That's why.* I have to think for the both of us. I've got to be responsible for this ship or else it's heading right into the rocks by the siren's call of our own out-of-check libidos and plain old desperation to not be alone.

This kid deserves more than me.

I realize that's a big statement to make about someone I just met. But perhaps we both have that uncanny ability to know a person in a short amount of time. Faces pass by my bar, a hundred a night, and I know desperation. I know the sting of need that lives beyond wet, drunken eyes. I know well-intentioned expressions. I know greedy ones. I know bad, bad boys with one thing in mind. I know boys with many things in mind—and I know Seany isn't one of them.

He's worth my time. He's worth my stress. He's worth my overthinking and my sleeplessness and my curiosity.

And if I have any hope of giving him the happiness he deserves, I need to do the one thing I can't stomach to do.

I need to let him go.

Y'know, some bullshit about if a bird truly loves you, set it free and hope it doesn't land on the wrong power line.

"You still can't sleep, can you?"

I didn't know he's still awake. "Go to sleep, Seany."

"I can't when you can't."

I chuckle. "Don't be stubborn."

"You're all stiff. Not in the good way."

"Seany ..."

"Like trying to snuggle with a filing cabinet." He slips onto his back in my arms, facing me. "Is this about the whole Monday hotel thing?"

"The what ...?"

"You said you were going to search for hotel rooms on Monday using your island favors. Said you'd do it so I can have my own space or whatever."

I completely forgot about that arrangement. "Oh."

"Is that what's on your mind? And you forgot about all the extra stuff going on this week, so you're worried there won't be vacancies or something?"

"No. I ..." He has my mind twisted around now. "I thought you wanted to stay here with me."

"I do."

"Then why would I be thinking about hotel rooms?"

"How am I supposed to know? Something's on your mind and you're leaving me to, like, figure it out all night like a puzzle. Are you having second thoughts about me staying here? You gonna kick me out in the morning?"

"No."

"You sure? A heads-up would be nice, y'know."

I sit up and peer down at him. "Seany, I'm not kicking you onto the streets. I will never do that. I told you."

"Then what's going on?"

"Do you really want to go to the thing tomorrow?"

The sudden question has Seany staring at me blankly. "I ... Huh? Do I what?"

"You heard me. Do you want to go to the bonfire and the street fair or not? Honest answer. Ignore what I said or how I might've reacted in front of the arcade earlier."

He doesn't answer.

I take that as one. "We're going, then."

"What?"

"The street fair and the bonfire. I said I wanted you to find your family here, right? I want you to be happy. So ... I'm making the decision for us. We're going out tomorrow night. You'll get to meet everyone who matters on the island. And also probably a lot of people who don't."

He turns away, peering up at the ceiling, looking lost.

I put a hand on his chest and give it a gentle rub. "You will have a good time. And if you don't, well, then I'll be there to take you out for late night tacos or whatever the hell you call a good Monday night."

"Hmm," is all he says.

I frown at him. "You wanted to go, right? See the guy you met before? Toby? You said he and his boyfriend wanted to hang out with you."

He takes a minute. "Well, yeah, I guess."

I lift an eyebrow. "You guess?"

"Toby said his boyfriend has a booth or something. He was being nice to me. I guess I should, like, support him or his boyfriend or whatever."

I thought it was what he secretly wanted to do.

Now he sounds like I'm twisting his arm.

I study the expression on Seany's face—or rather, the abyssal lack of any. Was I wrong? Does he prefer not to go out? Is it all too much too soon?

Seany might still need to build a sense of security here. He needs to build a sense of home. A sense of belonging.

Is bringing him right into the literal fire going to undo everything we've built over the weekend? Is he going to fall apart, get spooked, and run away forever?

Maybe the answer isn't to set the bird free after all. Especially if his wings are damaged—or simply tired of flying from tree to tree. Seany needs nurturing. He needs to be cared for. Looked after. Tended to.

He needs to feel safe here in our nest—*with me*.

So I face him. "Y'know, we also don't have to—"

"We'll go out tomorrow night, then," he cuts me off with a shrug. "Sounds like fun. We'll stuff our faces and look at art." He rolls onto his side. "Goodnight, Coop."

He drifts right to sleep—and I'm back to not knowing anything at all.

CHAPTER 12

SEANY

SUNLIGHT POURS IN THROUGH THE GLASS STOREFRONT.

And the mannequin stares at me from its faceless face through a pair of knockoff sunglasses.

"You lost?"

I turn to the store attendant: a tanned beach bum with a loose, unbuttoned Hawaiian shirt hanging on a tall skeletal frame, dead-eyed, who looks as if he either got twenty minutes of sleep last night or is high as hell.

Surprisingly, he asks the question with sincere concern, as if truly believing I'm lost and need help finding home.

Maybe I am still lost.

Maybe I am still finding home.

Have I forgotten how to make friends? How to care? At one point, I thought meeting nice guys like Toby and his boyfriend would have been the answer to my prayers. Now it feels like a nuisance. Working the bar last night kept me busy and gave me purpose. Hanging out with Coop in his house makes me feel safe and happy.

I thought I wanted to hang out with Toby tonight.

Now I can't even pick between this shirt or that one, as I stare at the stupid mannequin in the sunlight pouring in through the giant windows.

I pull a shirt off the rack. "I'll take one of these."

The afternoon speeds by as I drift from store to store along one of the wide streets cutting down the heart of Dreamwood Isle. I didn't realize how choosy I'd be. After all, this isn't technically my money I'm spending. I have to do actual math as I slowly whittle down the amount of cash Coop gave me to spend on a wardrobe while he does things at the bar. I thought he'd want to shop with me, but he said it was good for my self-confidence to do this on my own.

I wasn't sure I understood his answer. It felt a little bit demeaning somehow. But maybe it was also honest.

I guess I need to do things on my own, too.

I'm not Cooper's pet.

"Is there a clearance rack?" I ask an older lady working at another store down the road that smells like cinnamon.

She squints at me over a pair of readers. "It's a thrift store, hon, everything's clearance."

I bite my lip and consider two different pairs of shorts. The color of one of them reminds me of a pair I used to have back home.

So of course I put that right back on the rack and lift the other in the air. "I'll take one of these."

I want *nothing* of this new life to remind me of home.

I want to redefine what 'home' means.

I want it to be Cooper. I want it to be Dreamwood Isle. I want it to be these beaches. These new friends. To be the sunrise every morning I will never get used to. To be weird stores that smell like cinnamon.

I want my new home to be everything I'm not familiar with. Strange things. New things. Exciting things.

I want it to be every smile I wake up with.

Every smell of something frying in the pan.

Each grain of sand that gets caught between my toes.

"I'll take this, please," I say, pulling a lime green tank top off the rack. I've never been a lime green tank top kind of guy. Here, I can be. "And one of these, too."

Coop told me to meet him at the bar for a ride home after I was finished shopping. By the time I get there, it's late in the afternoon, and I look like I've had quite the day with seven different shopping bags in hand, stuffed with clothes. He waits for me on the front steps, gazing off at the beach through his shades. Then he spots me. "There you are."

I give my bags a wiggle. "Amazing how far you can stretch a dollar or two in this town."

"Especially when you avoid the boardwalk and the tourist shops like I told you." He takes most of the bags from me, lightening my load. "Ready to head back?"

"Didn't you need some help here at the bar?" I ask as I peer around him through the window. I spot Mars standing at the counter chatting with Chase and another bartender. The three of them seem in the middle of listening to a story someone is excitedly telling them when Mars glances over and sees me. She squints questioningly, observes me for all of five long seconds, then turns away.

I frown, wondering if something's up.

"Everything's covered for now," insists Coop. "Extra help is coming in, just in case we get any spillage from the Pride stuff on Cassanova. I'll have my phone on me."

"Oh." Cooper puts an arm around me and guides me away from the bar as I continue trying to get one last peek through the window at Mars.

When we're back at his place, I dump my spoils on his bed to inspect what I got.

Coop frowns. "No shoes?"

"Mine are just fine," I insist. "And shoes are expensive as hell. They'd blow half the budget alone. Besides, if I'm gonna be a beach bum now, I better get used to being in cheap flip-flops or barefoot."

"What about underwear?"

I glance at the clothes, realizing I'd forgotten. "I ... I'll just ... I've got the pairs you lent me, and—"

"You need underwear, too, Seany."

I roll my eyes. "Yes, *Dad*."

He shoots me a sharp look.

I realize quickly he doesn't find that as amusing as I did. "Sorry. I ... I can get everything I missed tomorrow. And I'm paying you back for all of this, by the way," I remind him. "What you gave me today is a *loan*."

"No, it wasn't."

"Yes, it was. I'm working at your bar now. I'm going to earn all of this like a grown adult. Which I am. I'm ..." I grab a shirt and start folding it. "I'm a grown adult."

He quirks an eyebrow. "A grown adult who folds his clothes *before* washing them?"

I toss the shirt back onto the bed. "I don't know what I'm doing. I'm gonna go take a shower, if that's alright."

"Of course."

I head for the bathroom, then stop at the door.

Have I gotten too comfortable too quickly?

"Um ... Coop?"

"Yeah?"

I face him. "Just wanted to say ... thanks."

His eyes search mine for a while. Then he shrugs. "For what?" He gives me a little smile, then turns away to start gathering clothes off the bed. After watching him briefly, I slip into the bathroom, shut the door, twist on the shower, then stare at my face in the mirror for five long minutes.

Then I'm standing under the water staring at the wall a lot longer than five minutes, letting the white noise of the shower drown out everything.

And as I twist off the water at the end of my shower, I have finally come to a decision.

The old Seany is gone.

I'm going to be a new man here in Dreamwood Isle.

I'm going to be—"Sean," I tell Coop when I'm drying off later, nothing but a towel around my waist. "Just Sean."

He appears surprised. "Really?"

"Yep." I fish a comb out of his drawer and run it through my hair as I study myself in the mirror. "Sean is what I go by now. It's decided."

He crosses his arms and leans against the doorframe.

I glance at him. "You don't like it?"

"I like and support all your decisions."

The way he worded that seems strange. "Are you still annoyed I forgot to get underwear, socks, and shoes?"

"Not annoyed at all."

"You wanted me to spend all your cash on Nikes and jockstraps? I saw jockstraps," I add, lowering my voice. "I saw stores full of tiny colorful bikinis, glittery thongs, and jockstraps."

"That would be one of the stores I suggested *avoiding*. And regardless of what you insist, you don't have to pay back anything."

"So you like just giving it all away? Won't let me work for it? Do you get off on this or something?" I push on. "Letting me spend all your money? Pampering myself? You want to spoil me, Cooper?"

"Do I look like one of those?"

"Cash daddies don't have any kind of look. They can look like anyone."

"Cash daddies?? No, I don't 'get off' on it."

"But you like me spending your money?"

"I like you having the experience of buying something in a store."

"Instead of stealing?"

"And of having clothes," he goes on like he didn't hear me. "*Options* of clothes for you to own and keep and wear."

"Clothes I will pay for," I insist.

"I just want you to feel more human. To get all of your confidence back. I love watching you transform from what you were Friday to ... what you're meant to be. Whether Seany or Sean." He smiles. "I like watching you."

My towel chooses this moment to gently unravel itself and drop to the floor.

Standing at the mirror naked, I shrug as I continue to comb my hair. "You said you like watching me. Go ahead."

Cooper has already averted his eyes.

I peer at him. "It's kind of adorable, you looking away like that."

"Can you put your towel back on, please?"

"Seriously? We've had sex. You've done a hell of a lot more than just *look* at all this."

"Seany …"

"It's *Sean*," I remind him, "and fine, I'll go ahead and put my towel back on, if it bothers you so damned much."

"Thank you." He waits. "Is it on?"

"Yep."

He looks at me again.

The towel is still very much on the floor, and I am still very much naked. "I lied," I answer playfully, grinning.

He looks away again with a sigh. "Sean …"

"Look, if you want me to live with you, and you want to take care of me so badly …" I toss the comb onto the counter and saunter right up to him. "You're gonna have to deal with the fact that I might wanna be naked around you from time to time. Hey, look at me."

Coop looks me in the eyes.

Only the eyes.

"Touch me."

He squints. "What?"

128

"Put your hands on me. Touch me."

"Sean …"

"I give you permission. Is that what you want? I give you permission to put your hands on my body." As soon as he starts to protest, I slap a finger to his lips. "Coop, this is the other side of that promise, y'know."

His eyebrows pull together. "Promise …?" he murmurs, his lips moving under my finger.

"Yeah. The one I made, and the one you made. You told me to keep my doors open. I told you not to pity me. And part of not pitying me is treating me like anyone else. Not some boy or fragile kid. Not some dudesel in distress."

"Dudesel??"

"Why don't you keep *your* doors open, too?" I take his hands and pull them around my body. "I think a man like you needs to practice what he preaches. You should keep your doors open, too." I slide his hands further down my back—landing them right on my bare ass. "*Wide* open."

Coop frowns. "You're trouble, Sean, you know that?"

"I'm getting hard."

"I know. I can feel it against my—"

"Why do you sound so tense, Coop? Does your job got you all stressed out? Put your hand on my dick. I'll put my hand on yours. Maybe we can relieve all the weird tension you're keeping in your body before we go out tonight."

"Seany …"

"There you go, slipping up with my name again." I put my hand between his legs and take a big fistful of Cooper. He grunts and scrunches up his face. "Mmm, feels like I'm not the only one." His eyes rock back as I massage him. "I think I might start calling you Coopy every time you slip."

His fingers slowly start to curl around my ass cheeks.

I'm winning this arm wrestle, bit by bit.

I lean into his ear, bringing my lips close. "*Just give in.*" I give his earlobe a little lick. "*I know you wanna.*"

For a moment, I've got him.

I own him.

Then his hands drag up my back, reach my shoulders, and gently push me away. He smiles at my confused face. "I would be happy to stay in, have fun with you, and enjoy whatever mischief you're trying to inspire here. But if we start, we'll never leave the house, and you'll miss out on making new friends, checking out the street fair, and—"

"We can do both," I cut him off. "We can do it all."

"One thing at a time. Pace yourself."

"But I—"

His hand slides up to my hair, caressing it, then brings his lips to my forehead for a kiss. He smiles patiently at me. "I know you're horny, Sean. You're young and full of hot, pumping blood. I was your age once."

"Please tell me you and I are *not* having a daddy-son talk when I'm standing in front of you, naked and hard."

"This island has a way of giving you exactly what you ask for. And it will never run out of supply. It will satisfy you until you're drowning in its shores." He gently touches my cheek, stroking it with a thumb, as if wiping away tears that aren't there. "It's the best advice I can give, and you won't know it for years. Pace yourself."

My jaw tightens.

"Don't pout," he adds.

"I'm not *pouting*," I growl, crossing my arms. Then I uncross them. "You *sure* you don't wanna have any fun at all before we go out? My dick is throbbing."

"Pace yourself." He kisses my forehead again, then slips away from me, heading down the hall to the kitchen.

I swear, if he says "pace yourself" one more time …

An hour later when we leave the house, I'm honestly still frustrated about it. Not only is Coop acting weird, but suddenly he has slammed his big foot on the brakes of my sexual advances. How else am I supposed to take this? Is he not into me anymore? Is the magic gone, just like that?

Was it a mistake to walk with him on the boardwalk?

To try and fulfill his dream?

I'm afraid of what's going on in Cooper's mind right now. Whatever he isn't telling me. The thing he fears. The thing he's trying to stop from happening. His worries.

I thought I knew him a figurative second ago.

Now I'm so fucking lost.

I can't get settled into something nice again, only to find out it was all an elaborate illusion meant to give me a false sense of security. I don't want any more rugs pulled out from under me. I have lost enough rugs and fell on my ass enough times thanks to life's dickhead moves.

"You can smell the street food already," remarks Coop as we stroll along the sidewalk together, making our way.

The worst part is that he looks so good tonight. He's not even all that dolled up. Just an understated t-shirt, fitted to his pecs, tight on his shoulders and sleeves. Pair of jeans that make his ass look so good. His short hair has that hot and lazy look to it, like his sexiness is just an accident.

And I'm not allowed to have any fun with that tonight?

What the fuck kind of torture is this?

"Yeah," I answer back. "Smells yummy."

"Hope you're hungry, because I'm buying you one of everything."

As we come up onto Cassanova Street, it actually isn't the food we find first. Lining both sides of the road are kiosks, booths, and tables of arts and crafts—as well as a lot more people than I expected for a Monday night. The street is lit from one end to the other by crisscrossing strands of lights hanging overhead, creating a canopy of stars under which we walk as we stroll past the vendors.

Everyone knows Cooper. He gets waved at by nearly every vendor or booth as we pass by. Being the owner of the main bar on the island, of course it makes sense that everyone knows his face.

I get some looks, too. Weird looks. "Who's that?" sorts of looks. I just keep my hands in the pockets of my shorts (one of the new pairs I bought today) and walk by Coop's side, keeping quiet and feeling a little weird.

My quiet trend continues whenever Cooper approaches a booth to make small talk with a friend. "You torched the glass yourself? I love the colors. This is Sean, by the way."

He introduces me to everyone we meet, too.

And we meet a lot of people.

"Hey, Jen, how's it going? This beaded jewelry is incredible. Your attention to detail improves every day." I feel Cooper pat my back. "This is Sean. Sean, this is Jen."

"Sean, come and meet Lee. He makes really cool art with nothing but recycled cans and wire hangers."

"Hey, Sean, check out Hudson's stuff. I think he's just a few years older than you. Hudson, this is Sean."

"Charlie, hey. This is my friend Sean."

"Sean, this is Ollie."

"Ray, meet Sean."

"Asher."

"Jackson."

"Emile."

"Javier."

"Sean, I want you to meet—"

Honestly, my mind can only hold so many names. If I was quizzed right now, I probably couldn't even remember my own. My face started hurting sixteen people ago, and I can't even tell you if I'm smiling anymore. I just nod with a flat face in lieu of nearly anything—verbal greetings and handshakes included. Several times I keep looking around for that Toby guy, but with the weird street lighting and all the people around us, I'd be surprised just to find my own reflection in a window.

"Oh, you'll want to try one of these," says Coop as we stop by a booth selling corndogs. We've finally found our way to the food. "Seriously, best thing you've ever put in your mouth. Finn told me once it's a special recipe with the batter. These corndogs are from the Hopewell Fair. Finn is a friend of mine, his family owns the harbor. Meet Aaron, the guy who doesn't burn the corndogs."

"Takes skill," mumbles the messy-haired, lanky Aaron, who looks stoned out of his mind. "Hey, are you hiring at the bar? I might want a new job. Don't tell Mr. Marty."

Coop chuckles at that. "You trade jobs too fast, Aaron. You should pick something and stick it out. Did you try the dog?" he asks me quietly. I take a bite, then realize it's hot as fuck and start blowing. "Sorry, they're fresh out of a vat of lava. Thanks for the dogs! Give my best to Finn!"

"Okay, but we, like, never see each other," he answers lamely to our backs as we head off.

We've taste-tested about seven different things by the time we reach the north end of the street, where I spot the Hopewell Fair in the distance, its colorful lights glowing against the dark horizon, now that the sun has set.

I need a minute. "Coop, I gotta take a leak." I point at a corner store nearby, stealing the opportunity. "I'll be right back. Hold this." I put my stick of cotton candy in his hand as he stands there bewildered and push my way into the store. Then I beeline for the public bathrooms in the back.

Once inside, I stand at the mirror and catch my breath.

This would be the second time tonight I've decided to keep myself company with my own reflection.

And after all that's going on tonight and the way he's treating me, it's more obvious than ever.

Cooper is trying to pawn me off.

He wants me to make friends. Find someone else. Be done with him and his hospitality. No longer need his help.

And if I'm wrong and he truly doesn't mind me staying at his place, then something else has to be off. He's feeling less intensely about me than I am of him. He senses my dependency on him. He's "just being nice".

In which case, he may still want to pawn me off.

Even if he doesn't admit it himself.

This is driving me crazy.

"*Ugh, I shouldn't have eaten it,*" moans a voice from one of the closed stalls, almost unintelligible.

I politely decide to ignore that voice, twist on a faucet to spare him the humiliation of whatever he's attempting to accomplish with his bowel system, then resume staring at the mirror in frustration.

That's when the bathroom door opens and someone else comes in.

A twenty-something guy I happen to recognize.

He smirks like he knows something as he struts toward the counter. "Hey, hey, bro … Thought you bailed."

It's like a switch in my brain. The second I see his slim, pale face, blond stubble, and twitchy eyes, I'm just a kid on the streets again looking out for my own with no one to trust. He goes by Ice, appropriately, considering his dead, grayish eyes, which a kinder person might call ice-blue.

"Still here," I answer vaguely.

"Not where you usually are, though."

He's talking about the east end of town by the bluffs, where I'd been finding spots to sleep whenever it felt safe and I didn't feel like sleeping at the park, or the park was too crowded with other people. I thrust my hands under the running faucet to wash them, pretending it's what I'm here to do, ignoring him.

He leans against the counter and folds his arms. "Tell me, c'mon, what's been up? You got in somewhere? What kinda sweet deal did you score?"

"Nothing."

"Haven't seen you since last Thursday, and all you got to say to your best friend is 'nothing'?"

He is *not* my best friend, but I won't say that and risk getting him angry. He's an unbalanced guy. Short temper. Irritable between his fixes. I wish I could have nothing to do with him ever again, but when you're on your own with no roof over your head, bouncing from spot to spot every night, you learn how to use every relationship you got. The more people respect you on the streets, the safer you are.

If "safe" is a word I can ever trust again.

"C'mon," he presses me. "Is it something I can squeeze into? Some beach cougar you're hooking up with? Some lonely rich bitch made you a houseboy?"

"Nah, nothing like that."

"Just tell me, man."

I have to say something he'll believe. "I'm having luck with this round of tourists, that's all."

"Bullshit."

"And a street fair with lots of yummy free food ..."

He slides close to me and nudges my side. "Are you taking advantage of all the gay shit going on? Getting in with one of these gay dudes? Buttering someone up?"

"No."

"Does your deal ... have to do with that hunky older guy outside?"

My blood turns into ice. "Back off."

"So it *does* have to do with him. I saw you out there. I saw you with that guy. That's how I know."

I face him full-on. "I said back off."

"Hey, whoa." He lifts his hands and laughs. "That's no way to treat your best friend! C'mon, I'm just chatting with you. Catching up. Don't you wanna know what *I've* been up to all weekend?"

"If you saw me with him, then why are you pretending like you don't know what's going on? Asking me about beach cougars and rich bitches?"

"Because I was giving you an opportunity to tell me the truth. Obviously you failed. You don't trust your best friend. We've gotta work on that."

I don't even bother drying my hands. "I gotta go."

The moment I try to get around him, he blocks my way. "He into threesomes?" Ice invades my space again, leaning in close. "Why can't you work me in, dude? He rich? You think we can score off of him?"

Suddenly the roles have reversed and I'm the one who is protecting Cooper. "I'm not with him."

"Don't lie."

"I'm just checking out the street fair. Y'know half of the food booths give out free samples, right?"

His voice hardens. "I said don't lie to me."

The change of his tone makes my confidence break. I know how he can get. Conversations become a minefield.

Any misstep or wrong word can get dangerous quickly. I learned that lesson the first day I met him, same day I got off a bus with an old lady and her husband.

An old lady whose offer I declined still hangs over me like a ghost, haunting me with what-ifs and fading dreams.

Unless she was just another trap.

A call to the police. A call to my dad. A call to Jesus, to a camp for troubled kids, to some secret Hell she had planned for me.

I may never know.

"I'm not lying," I gently assure him, my voice losing all its edge. "There really *are* free samples out there."

"That's not what I meant and you know it. Don't play dumb. What is it you got going on with the bartender guy?"

He played dumb—and played me. He knows Coop's a bartender. Either he has been watching me all weekend or recognizes Coop from the bar.

This whole thing just went from bad to worse.

What can I tell him that sounds reasonable? Obviously Mr. Sherlock here knows more than he's telling me, so I can't just fib my way out of this. I can't afford for him to catch me in another lie. He's scary and unpredictable.

Before I can start my sentence, the noise of a flushing toilet fills the whole restroom like a hurricane, then one of the stall doors flies open.

And out comes Toby.

Toby, the person who knows I'm a liar and a thief.

Toby, who just heard all of this.

Toby, who probably thinks I'm the scum of the earth now, taking advantage of lovable, giving Cooper.

As if just now becoming aware of us, Toby puts on a bright smile. "Hey there!" he greets me as he twists on a faucet and starts vigorously washing his hands. Ice and I have drawn silent, watching him. "Phew, that spicy burrito totally hit wrong. That'll be the last time I ever gamble on habanero." He flicks his hands at the sink several times to dry them, then throws an arm around a very stunned me. "Ready to get back out there, bud? Vann's waiting for us."

Without even a moment to acknowledge Ice or the odd expression on his face, Toby scoops me straight out of the restroom and into the store.

As we pass through the aisles, I start panicking. "Toby, I ... I don't know how much you, uh, heard, but I swear it wasn't what it sounded like. That guy is a—"

"Don't sweat it, bud. It isn't my business. I don't need to know."

"Really, I'm not taking advantage of Cooper. That guy is a crazy bum who wouldn't leave me alone when I used to sleep at the park, and—" I freeze. I never told Toby I'm homeless. He knows nothing. "I mean when I first came to town. From San Antonio. The guy just found me and—"

"It's okay, it's okay, no need to explain."

I feel like there's *every* need to explain. But the more I say, the more there is to explain. "Toby ..."

"You encounter weirdoes here all the time, especially when big events are going on. Vann and I have barely been here a month or so and it's the first lesson we learned."

Did he miss the part about me sleeping in the park? Is he really so unfazed by things, or did he not catch the very clear implication? "Yeah," I decide to agree, dismissing my worries. "Weirdoes. Right."

We spill through the sliding doors of the corner store, returning to the streets. I spot Cooper right away, chatting with a man at a nearby table, my cotton candy stick still in his hand. He doesn't see me just yet, but from the look on his face, I hesitate to approach. He seems stressed.

So am I.

Just one encounter in the bathroom and I feel my little paradise crumbling in the palms of my hands.

Was I a fool to believe any of this could actually last?

CHAPTER 13

COOPER

"I'M JUST TELLING YOU, MY FRIEND, THE ROOM'S YOURS."

I feel like I'm talking circles around Taj. "And I very much appreciate that, but like I said, the situation is—"

"Different, yes, I have ears, but need I remind you, my dear friend, that *you* are the one who came to me not a handful of nights ago in desperate need of a *room*-room. Half the Sunnyview cleared out overnight, and I'm able to more than accommodate the cutie now."

If my face was any redder right now … "Taj, I'm not looking for a 'room-room' anymore. I never was. I needed a room for Seany to stay in, and—"

"Oh, what a precious name."

My jaw tightens. "But I have since decided to let him stay at my place. Things are different now."

"Different." Taj squints skeptically at me. "Are we on the same page, dear Cooper? It feels as if we are reciting passages from very different books."

"Then let me be as clear as possible: Thank you. You are a good friend. The room is appreciated. However, it is not needed anymore. The boy is staying with me."

"Under your protective wing. You're his daddy now. I get it. I heard the fairytale." Taj sighs. "But boys grow up, dear Cooper."

I stare at him, lost. "Grow up?"

"It's the last week of Pride. There are boys aplenty all over town. How are you going to support his needs when he wants to bring one home? That tiny one-bedroom house of yours is really going to accommodate him? Where will they make babies? Your bed? Kick you out onto your own couch so they can have private boom-boom time? This is a fairytale you're spinning, Cooper, and I say this with love and concern for your wellbeing. For all your age, you are still so very young in your mind, believing in such dreams. The kid needs his independence."

"I *know* that," I snap.

Taj's eyes go big.

I sigh and pinch the bridge of my nose. "Sorry."

"Nothing to apologize for. I'm not a frail little doily." He gives me a brisk pat on the shoulder. "The room will be there tonight. Likely all week. You have my number if you change your mind. Now if you'll excuse your dear friend, he is going to sample a seafood stand he's been eyeballing all night. It's anyone's guess whether I'm eyeballing the food or the adorably-dressed vendor. Best of luck to you." He strolls away with that, leaving me on the curb.

I shouldn't have snapped at Taj. I know he's trying to help, and he's giving me exactly what I asked for.

Still, something about this night has my nerves feeling wire-tight. Like I'm doing it all wrong. Like I'm making the biggest mistake of my life.

The more I think about encouraging Sean's freedom and independence, the more I cling.

I've never been so conflicted about anything.

"Hey."

I turn. Sean has returned from his pee break. He looks so cute in his new pastel beach shirt, half unbuttoned with a tank underneath, and matching shorts. It takes everything in me not to just scoop him up in my arms and race home with him, breaking all of my own principles and claiming him as mine.

Then I notice the Toby kid standing a few paces behind him. He waves. "Hey there! I don't think we have officially met, despite coming to your bar a few times, but I'm—"

"Toby, of course." I shake his hand. "Whenever there's a new citizen, word gets around fast." I notice Sean keeps glancing over his shoulder back at the corner store, arms crossed tightly over his chest. He seems antsy. "I know all my customers who come in for everything *but* the alcohol."

Toby chuckles. "Yeah, not quite old enough, yet."

"Don't pretend like you haven't drank before," I tease Toby while keeping an eye on Sean, who can't stand still.

"Just a sip here and there, I swear! I'm not really a fan. My boyfriend loves wine. Apparently his mom has a whole cellar situation happening back home in Spruce. Speaking of which, I'd better go check on Vann. I left him alone at his table. We haven't sold much." Toby pouts, then nudges Sean, who snaps out of his restless daze. "Come stop by our table when you got a minute, alright? I want you to see how fucking cool Vann's stuff is."

Sean nods too quickly. "Yeah, of course, great." He pastes on a tightened smile. "Will do."

"See y'all later!" Toby gives us both a vague wave, then hurries off back down the street.

Before I can say anything, Sean takes the stick of blue cotton candy out of my fingers, hooks his arm into mine, and steers me away down the street like we're in a hurry. I study the side of his face as he stares into the cotton candy like he's looking for his future in a crystal ball.

What the hell has gotten into him?

145

"Did you run into him in the store?" I ask.

Sean's eyes flash. "Who? What?"

"Toby."

"Oh." He takes a big bite of his cotton candy. Some of it sticks to his lips, which he licks off before answering. "I ran into him in the bathroom, yeah. He was having a bad situation with a burrito. Oh … That was our secret. Oops."

I smirk. "Probably from Mars's mom's taqueria. They make them nice and spicy. Longer he lives here, the more he'll get used to it. Mars isn't really an employee of mine. She just hops in to help now and then, or whenever she's bored and doesn't want to work under her mom."

"Cool," he says absently before chomping off more of the cotton candy and staring blankly ahead.

I frown at him. "You alright?"

"Yeah." He still doesn't look at me.

I glance over my shoulder at the vendors across the street. We have made our way back to the art area, by the looks of it. My mind is so twisted around from my convo with Taj and my own self-doubts, I can't help but wonder if meeting up with Toby has Sean thinking things again.

Is he sticking by my side out of obligation?

Does he actually want to hang out with Toby instead?

"Toby's a nice guy," I point out lightly, throwing the fishing line into the water.

"Yeah."

"Genuine. Kind-hearted. Apparently doesn't drink," I add with a choked chuckle. He doesn't react. I give him a nudge. "You want to check out his boyfriend's work?"

"Hmm?" The question stirs him. "Oh, you mean now?"

"Why not?"

He nods. "Sure, yeah, we can … we can do that."

And now for the real test: "Well, I got a call from the bar while you were in the restroom. I'm apparently needed for something, so—"

"You are?"

"Yeah. Why don't you find Toby and hang out with him for a while? Check out his boyfriend's artwork. This is what you wanted to do anyway, right?"

Sean meets my eyes. There's a question behind them he doesn't seem ready to ask.

I give him a pleasant, encouraging smile—as pleasant and encouraging as I can manage. "Maybe they'll hit up the bonfire afterwards. It's just down the beach from the house, if you want to head back later on."

"*If* I want to head back?"

"I don't know. Maybe you'll have fun with your new friends and want to crash with them. Depends on how you feel, I guess. That's the thing with Dreamwood," I go on as I look him over, keeping that smile on my face. "You can never predict what each day will bring … what shiny new opportunity will wash up on the shore."

Sean looks off for a moment, appearing pensive. "Oh, okay," he finally says.

"This is that whole 'keep your doors open' thing."

He bites his lip. When he looks at me, his whole tone changes. "Can we just go instead?"

I lift my eyebrows, surprised. "What?"

"I can come with you to the bar to help," he insists, a note of desperation in his voice. "Then we can, like, just go back to your place. I've seen enough. I don't need to hang with anyone or do any bonfire or anything."

What the hell is going on? "Sean?"

Just then, a voice calls out: "Hey, guys! Over here!"

We turn to find Toby at a table with displays showing off what appears to be artfully illustrated demons, angels, and strange monsters with twisty horns and knobby wings. Toby waves ecstatically at us, a cheery smile on his face.

I ignore all of that and put a hand on Sean's shoulder. "You alright?"

Whatever panic lived on his face vanishes. "Uh, never mind. It's nothing. I'll hang with Toby and his boyfriend. Everything's fine."

He slips from my grasp and cuts across the street toward Toby's table. I watch as the two reunite, and Toby happily takes the reins, showing off his boyfriend's art. I'm left in the middle of the street among the crowd, watching, feeling like a lurking ghost peering in through a window.

I'm haunted by that moment the whole way to the Easy Breezy. Twice, I stop and reconsider going back for Sean, then remind myself of my own promise. When I ascend the handful of steps to the doors of the bar, I stop yet again, a tangle of thorny misgivings tightening in my stomach.

"Uh, boss man, you alright?"

I flinch at the sound of Chase's voice, coming from one of the front windows, open to let in the air. His sandy-blond hair is unexpectedly combed neatly tonight, and his eyes look as calm and languid as the ocean.

For a moment, I can forget this whole weekend. I can go back to my normal life. No commitments. No worries. No pressures. Everything as easy and as breezy as it should be. The only responsibilities are my dear plants on my back porch. No confusing boys in my life. No questions.

I'm ashamed to say how appealing that sounds—the comfort of my boring life I had before I met Sean.

"Boss?"

I keep losing myself to my thoughts. "Yeah, I'm here."

"Why? It's dead as hell over here, nothing going on."

The phone call from the bar was a stupid fib. It was an excuse to give Sean his freedom. Now I feel as stupid and flimsy as the fib.

"Just wanted to check on some things," I mutter tiredly before letting myself in.

"Oh, okay. I've got everything handled, though."

149

"No biggie." There are only a handful of customers—a guy and a girl taking turns playing darts, a couple of guys chatting and sipping on beer at a table, and a lone man at the bar, who looks like he's about to fall asleep over his glass of whiskey. "Did you send Mars off?"

"Never came in. Her mom needed her for something. Actually ..." Chase catches up to me as I round the counter to take a look at the register. "I have a question for you."

My mind is completely consumed with Sean. I barely have room for a thought of my own, let alone a question. Still: "Yeah, what is it?"

"I was wondering if you're considering raises again."

I quirk an eyebrow. "Raises? Really?"

"It's usually around this time of year that you give Ty and Dunc and August their evals, but things have been kind of crazy lately, and if you're planning on hiring the Seany kid, I know you'll need to rework some of the numbers ..."

"Wait, wait, wait."

"I just want to be prepared, alright? And I'd like you to not forget me in the storm of everything going on." Chase takes a breath. Clearly this has been weighing on his mind. "Anyway, I'll leave you be. Also, I *do* like the Seany boy. He's dedicated and keeps the place tidy way better than Ty or Duncan do. Can you watch the front for a sec? I need to take the *biggest* dump right now."

Hearing those words from that pretty face. "Alright."

Chase disappears faster than I can blink, and I take my position behind the counter. After washing glasses, sorting some bottles, and checking the register, I've run out of shit to do.

I shouldn't have left Sean.

No, I did the right thing, I argue with myself.

Why does it feel like shoving my kid off to college? Is this the tragic result of having let my heart collect dust for so long? The moment someone touches it, he owns it, and I am completely consumed by him.

For all I know, Sean is kicking it with Toby and Vann, laughing and getting to know each other, loving life and all its plethora of possibilities. He's realizing I was right. He's making friends with good people his age. When I see him, he will thank me for pushing him into the throng.

Even if it makes my eyebrow twitch involuntarily.

Even if prickles of jealousy and confusion run up and down my arms.

Even if I go fucking nuts worrying about him.

The man at the bar has fallen asleep, glass of whiskey forgotten. I reach for his bowl of nuts to refill it, then find myself lost in thought suddenly.

Nuts.

That's how this whole thing started.

Chasing a can of fucking nuts out of those doors and coming back with a whole lot more.

The doors open so quietly, I barely notice, peering up from the half-empty bowl still in my hand. In comes a man wearing a shirt buttoned almost to the neck, vertical stripes in alternating colors of burnt orange and cream, with bright white shorts. His skin is like peaches and cream, smooth and barely touched by the sun. Sunglasses sit atop his head of short brown hair, styled meticulously.

When his eyes meet mine, my world comes to a halt.

At first, I go into complete denial. *It's not him. How can it possibly be him? It's been ten years, maybe more, and he is long gone.* But upon seeing me, he has frozen to the spot, too. A mixture of excitement and worry fills his eyes, as if he regrets coming through the doors.

His name falls off my tongue. "Drake ...?"

He takes a deep breath, then walks about halfway up to the counter before stopping again. "Cooper. It's ... It's so great to see you after all this time."

I *did* see him the other day. I saw him outside the bar. I didn't imagine it. "What are you doing here?"

Drake bites his lip, glances at the couple playing darts to collect his thoughts, then faces me again. "I won some tickets to the Hopewell Fair Pride Festival. I ..." He almost laughs, then chokes it down. "I was going to give mine to someone else, but my friends really wanted to come, so ..." He thrusts his hands into his pockets. "I probably shouldn't have come, huh?"

To look at him and still see the lost eighteen-year-old in his youthful eyes. To still see the wild boy I danced with at the club. The boy who raced me from one end of the beach to the other before we crashed into the water with laughter. The boy I taught to surf. The boy who first made me see what it was like to commit to someone for longer than a weekend, who put an end to my partying days, who helped me explore the possibility of love. I was twenty-eight and lost. He was the boy who found me.

Then threw me away.

"I debated coming in several times," he admits, taking a few more steps toward the counter. "I kept talking myself out of it. Telling myself to stay away ... saying, 'Haven't I done enough to Cooper?' I'm surprised you can even look me in the face without wanting to punch it."

I drop my gaze to the half-empty bowl of nuts, lost.

"Of course. You would never punch me." Drake sighs. "You aren't the one who harms people. I am."

Am I supposed to feel sorry for him?

"It's the truth." He drops onto the bar stool across from me. "Look, I don't have to stay long. I just wanted to come and say hi. Well, no, that's a lie. I wanted to make sure you were happy. But every time I passed by, you were busy." He shrugs. "I guess keeping busy is a form of being happy. You were always such a hard worker, even back then."

Back then.

153

Those two tiny words carry a world within them—*back then*. So much pain and joy twisted around each other, it's impossible to untangle and tell them apart.

"I thought maybe we could talk." He's still looking at me, perhaps hoping I'll look back. "A lot has happened. I went to college and got that degree. Y'know, just like you said I should. Even graduated with honors."

Is this when I congratulate him? I stare at the counter, entirely unable to meet his eyes. My heart is pounding, but it's unclear whether with anger, hurt, or something else.

"Okay, I lied again," he says suddenly. "I'm not here with friends. I'm alone. Just myself. I bought a single ticket to the Pride thing at the fair, and I went this past weekend. Now my purpose here in Dreamwood Isle is over. You are my purpose now. Seeing you and ... and talking to you, I guess. I was supposed to go home last night. I booked my room for two more nights. I leave tomorrow morning."

"What do you want?" I ask.

"I don't know. I don't know, Cooper. Can you look at me, please?"

"Closure? Is that it? Is that what you came here for?"

"Talking is easier when you look at each other."

I pull my stony gaze off the counter and aim it at him.

Drake retracts, fear in his eyes.

"Does it feel easier now?" I ask coldly.

He lets out a shaky sigh. "Not really."

"What part of this is supposed to be easy, exactly? You want to know how I am? I'm alone. I'm bitter and broken. I pour myself into this bar because it's all I really have. This bar, and the people who care about me. You want closure? Too bad. You're going to have to live with what you did to me. Your actions have consequences, and when you carve out another man's heart for sport—"

"Cooper, that's not what—"

"—you have to know it *won't* be easy to look that man in the eye. You can't slither back into his hometown, into his bar, into his *life* and expect him to look you in the eye and give you the gift of closure. Who in their right mind welcomes back the demon who sucked out his soul?"

Drake's face twists irritably, for a second making him look exactly like the defiant, cocky eighteen-year-old who fled Dreamwood Isle.

"Bit dramatic, are we?" says Drake. "A demon? That's what I am?"

"You'd be dramatic too if you lived even a *second* of the hell I experienced after you left."

"I never said I was here for closure."

"What, then? A second chance? Not gonna happen."

He looks away. "This was a mistake."

"At least we agree there." I fold my arms. "Not exactly sure what you expected from me."

He shuts his eyes and goes quiet.

155

The fight flees my system, looking at him like that. His face reminds me of how he'd look when he fell asleep, but now he's got stubble and his face is fuller. I feel ten years younger. I feel less achy, less tired, less stressed. I really did live up to the name of this bar back then: easy breezy, not a worry on my mind, adrift on the raft of life.

The past can be the most seductive thing.

That's all Drake is: a walking, talking advertisement for my past.

"Maybe this *wasn't* a mistake," he says after a thought. He lays a hand on the counter and starts drumming a little rhythm with his fingers—a specific, familiar rhythm. "You deserve to unleash your anger. You've probably had it pent up in you all these years. No one else deserves it but me."

"If you came just to throw yourself a pity party ..."

"I'm angry at me, too. Ten-years-younger me. I wish I could go back and talk to him. Yell at him. Make him see. Wipe away all his youthful arrogance ..." His fingers drum harder. "Honestly, I want to *join* you in your anger. Vent *with* you. I have a lot of regrets. Yes, I will live with them forever, I can't change what I did. But if there's anything I can give you ..." His drumming stops. "It's knowing that the boy who hurt you is gone."

I'm finished listening to him. "You should have stuck with your first instinct. That this was a mistake. If you have no further business in Dreamwood, then goodbye."

"Cooper ..."

The bathroom door swings open with a bang, and out struts a very relieved-looking Chase, positively beaming. "*Man*, that was one epic dump." He comes right up to my side, oblivious to the tension. "Anyway, I've given it more thought, about the whole raise thing, and—Are you okay?"

I stare at him.

Drake stares at him.

Chase frowns, then notices Drake. "Oh! Sorry, sir. Am I ... interrupting something ...?"

Drake pulls his hand off the counter. "No. I was just on my way out." He looks at me. "I leave tomorrow morning. When I go, it's ... for the very last time. Sunnyview, room 424. Just to talk. If you want to free your heart from the chains I put on it. You deserve more." Then he slides off of the barstool and heads out without looking back.

I stare numbly at the door after it swings shut. Not a single thought seems to permeate the iron wall that was just erected in my mind. The man sleeping at the bar starts to snore. The couple playing darts break into laughter at some funny thing that happens during their game. The world just keeps moving, and all I can do is stare at that door.

"Boss? Did you, uh ... know that guy ...?"

I come to, grab the half-empty bowl off the counter, and refill it. "Not anymore."

CHAPTER 14

SEANY

AT FIRST, IT'S BORING.

Then it's crazy busy.

Toby's boyfriend's table is swarmed by a huge group of local college students who are apparently obsessed with his work. I step back and find myself just standing around picking at my fingernails and feeling useless. Vann isn't at all like I expected him to be, judging from Toby. With his wild black hair, earrings, sleeveless black shirt, torn skinny jeans, and spiked cuffs on his wrists, the guy looks like he plays lead guitar in a 90s cover band. It's no wonder his art is full of demons and monsters. But the longer I see the two of them together, the more I realize how perfectly they complement one another. Toby is the sweetness an artist like Vann needs to temper him. Vann is the wild side Toby needs to pull him out of his shell. Had Vann been on the beach that first day I met Toby, I doubt I would have made it out with that cash; something about Vann seems strong and protective, like he would never let his precious Toby be taken advantage of.

It makes me happy, but it also hurts a little, to watch the two of them together.

Then I think about the way Toby came to my rescue. It might be a good thing it was Toby I befriended and not Vann. Vann looks like the kind of guy who wouldn't have held back in planting a fist into Ice's face.

No, I haven't seen Ice again. But this island is only so big. It's inevitable I'll run into him again. Unless luck is on my side, he grows bored, and Dreamwood Isle becomes a memory for him.

Somehow, I doubt that'll happen.

Bad luck has a way of staying on my heels.

Toby keeps apologizing to me for the craziness while he juggles managing the customers and attending to (his very overwhelmed-looking) artist boyfriend. I remind him I can help, but he insists I just relax and enjoy myself.

I watch him count change for a customer.

Dollars slide from his hand to the table.

Counting them out one by one.

Dollars being folded up and slid neatly into a cash box.

Toby's eyes wandering to mine, smiling sweetly, then returning his attention to the customers.

That's about when I remember that just a few days ago, I stole from him. I admitted it, too. I remind myself of what he probably overheard in the bathroom between me and Ice—whether he believed it or not.

Is it possible he doesn't *trust* me to help him?

With the crowd of college students around the table, it seems to draw even more interest from random passersby. I keep finding myself stepping further back to make more room until soon, I'm on the sidewalk with my back against a lamppost, aloof and disconnected from it all.

I wonder if anyone would notice if I disappeared.

I decide to test that theory and walk away.

I only make it five steps. "Hey, Seany! Where are you going?" calls out Toby. "To get some food?"

I turn, surprised. "Uh ..."

"Oh, look!" Toby snatches one of the illustrations off the table and presses it to my chest, startling me. "Doesn't this look like my friend Seany here?"

I can't even see the artwork, but suddenly *I'm* the one who's now bombarded by their collegiate groupies, all of them staring at the picture, then me, then the picture. "Yes! He totally does!" shouts a girl. "Wow, totally!" "Is he the actual inspiration?" "He's *totally* the muse!" "Oh, I want a demon portrait of me done, too!"

I've gone from being invisible to being the only thing visible.

"Are you a model?" someone asks me.

I quirk an eyebrow. "Is that a joke?"

"Dude, what are your rates?" asks someone else, a guy with glasses and hot pink hair. "You've got a unique look."

"But also totally a classical look, right?" throws in a girl by his side, squinting at me like I'm the new piece of art she's analyzing. "His jawline is *impeccable*."

"Sweet, soulful eyes that tell so many stories."

"Yeah, and what a great frame!"

"Have you posed for an art class on campus before? I swear I've seen you."

"My roommate's in need of a model just like you ..."

The comments and questions fire at me nonstop. I keep shifting my focus, alarmed by all of the attention. "I don't know," I mutter to one person. "Rates? What the hell do you mean by that? Commission, huh? I'm not a model. I'm just—No, I've never been there before. No, I have no idea who that is. Uh, sorry, what was that about an agent?"

Clearly noticing that I'm drowning, Toby comes to my rescue by fielding the questions, taking over the crowd and redirecting them. I'm mercifully no longer the center of attention and feel instantly schooled for ever wanting to be noticed in the first place.

It's an hour later when the crowds have dissipated and the boys are packing up their stuff for the night. I take hold of the illustration, for the first time getting to see it myself. It looks like a guy our age, naked, crouched on top of a dresser with his knees hugged to his chest. Each drawer is partly open with different kinds of clothing spilling out— from jeans and tank tops to ballerina leotards to soccer socks to a fancy tuxedo jacket. From the little guy's back sprouts two giant bat wings, which are barely noticed upon first glance, looking as if they're just shadows spread over the wall. His face does admittedly bear a resemblance to mine, with his lost eyes, messy hair, and guardedness.

I wonder for a moment if this demon portrait is exactly me: A lost boy, wondering who he is, trying on a thousand different outfits, none of which seem to fit. So he's given up and wears nothing at all, letting his scary, beautiful bat wings spread. He has no idea where he fits in. Who to dress as. What to be.

"It's yours," says Toby.

I look up, startled. "What?"

"Vann already said it's okay. It's all yours. Consider it a gift from us to a new friend." Toby smiles.

I stare back at him, overcome. "Really? But you could sell this sometime this week and make … however much this was selling for."

"You can't put a price on that look in your eyes."

I blink, unsure what to say.

Toby smiles. "Hey, do you mind helping us carry some of this stuff back to our place before we hit up the bonfire? We live just around the corner, a little five or ten minute walk from here."

And to think that just a while ago, I was sure Toby had changed his mind about me and wanted nothing to do with a kid who steals money and sleeps in parks.

On the way to their house, Toby and Vann banter back and forth about their day and how it began so dismally, but ended on a high note. I mostly keep to myself, but I find myself smiling with them, feeling strangely purposeful. Their house is a colorful and quirky one just up the road from the beach. Inside, the furniture is as surprising and unpredictable as they are, bursting with art and color and personality. We spend a mere handful of minutes inside (to essentially dump everything by the door) before heading off as a happy trio down to the beach.

Before long, I'm standing around a bonfire among a modest crowd of guys and gals from the locals' end of the island. Toby tells me there are usually a lot more people at these things, so maybe everyone is still distracted with the Pride stuff going on all over the island, or are having their own house parties. I'm drinking from a bottle of off-brand carbonated lemonade I've never heard of before, along with Toby and Vann by my side, who start introducing me to some of the people around the fire. It's just like Cooper taking me down Cassanova Street; once one name is put into my head, it's shoved right out with another name. I can't keep anyone straight, but I smile and nod anyway, trying to be as comfortable as I can.

"Looks like you've got another enticing career option," teases Toby with a nudge into my ribs, "if modeling wasn't already on your radar."

It wasn't. It still isn't. I wouldn't dream of modeling for anyone or anything.

But still: "Yeah, I'm open to anything."

"The local college is a great place to find oddball gigs. The art departments are always needing people. Performing arts school, too. Not to mention the science building, where they do psychology experiments and train counselors with models and actors. Do you act? I'm an actor, kinda, sorta."

It was a pretty amazing experience, all of those college students being so fascinated with me for a moment. If my life had gone differently, I might be one of them right now, happily stressing over projects, commiserating with fellow classmates, studying for exams …

The dream of living a college life is thrilling suddenly.

It's also a possibility I would never have considered a week ago—a possibility I was sure I'd never know.

"Vann is a student there," Toby points out. "He can get

you a foot in the door if you want, I'm pretty sure."

"Thanks." I take another fizzy, lemony swig from the bottle. After a minute, I realize I can't help myself. "Hey, about that guy in that corner store restroom ..."

"Who? Oh, that weirdo? Nah, it's okay, Seany, really, you don't have to explain."

"I ran away from home." I take a moment to gather myself. "I-I'm homeless."

Toby faces me fully, all cheer fleeing his face at once, his eyes turning serious. I'm not sure whether this is him paying attention, or if he really didn't have any idea at all.

"You ..." He brings his voice down, despite likely no one else being able to hear us anyway. "You ran away from home? Really?"

"Yeah. It was a while ago. Right after New Year's."

Toby gasps. "You've been out there on your own since January?"

"Sort of. It's a long story. I've been staying with Coop since the weekend. I'm sorry I didn't tell you sooner. I've just been taken advantage of so many times, or tricked, or let down ... I never know who to trust. I've only recently arrived here to Dreamwood Isle a few weeks ago. I've been sleeping in the park or out by the east bluffs. It's how that guy knows me," I finally get to explain. "He's convinced I'm trying to win myself a sugar daddy or something with Cooper, like I'm just some street rat clawing his way up by any means possible. I'm not. I just want a normal life. I'm tired of the uncertainty, the looking over my shoulder—"

Toby tackles me with a hug at once, crushing away all of my words. I stare over his shoulder at the fire, paralyzed.

"I ... am *so* sorry, Seany. You've dealt ... with so ... so much. I am so ... so ... *so* sorry ..."

I squirm a bit in his hug, then give in, letting him hold me. I don't really know what to say.

He lets go suddenly and steps back. "Uh, sorry. I get a bit overly emotional."

"It's okay. It was ... uh ... nice, I think."

"Really, I'm so happy you found Cooper."

"Yeah, but ..." I sigh. "That guy from the restroom—his name's Ice, probably his street name—it's obvious he's been watching me, because he knows I've been with Coop. I don't want him to come after Coop, or to—"

"Nah, don't even think about that. If this Ice guy has a brain, he won't do anything to you or Coop. Everyone on the island knows Cooper. Even the police love the guy."

"Thanks."

"You've got me and Vann to protect you. And big bar boss Cooper can protect himself *and* you. I won't ask about your family or why you ran away. It isn't my business, and believe me, I know *all* about dysfunctional families. I ... kind of ran away from my own, but that was just for a day. My best friend Kelsey was once in a very similar situation to yours, then found herself bouncing from foster home to foster home. She was staying with us just last week, but went home to Spruce this weekend for one of her dads' birthdays, otherwise I would have introduced you two." He grimaces. "Sorry, I'm talking a lot. The point is, I'd never judge another person for their situation. Maybe someday we can trade stories and get to know each other better. But only in your own time. Just know that you're safe here and among friends, okay?" He hooks an arm around my neck, pulling me close like he's suddenly my big bro. "Here in Dreamwood, you'll always have a family. You have us."

I find myself smiling despite my pesky misgivings.

It might be a bumpy ride before I finally feel truly at home here. But people like Toby in my life sure make the transition that much easier.

I sure wish Cooper was with me right now.

I don't know what time it is when I say goodnight and break away from what remains of the bonfire. The wind is crazy strong as I walk down the coast by myself, my eyes jumping from house to house, looking for Cooper's beach-facing porch as my hair gets yanked in every direction. When I finally find the porch (and the plethora of potted plants that make it so easy to identify), I notice only one light on inside: his bedroom, its window facing the shore. I head up the sand to his steps, kick off my sandals, then let myself in through the back door.

In the dark living room, I hear the sound of his typing from the bedroom. After setting down the cardboard tube on the couch (which contains Vann's artwork, rolled up neatly courtesy of Toby, to be hung up later) I pass through the dark living room and down the short hall, stopping at Cooper's door. He's at his computer still in his clothes, a pair of glasses at the end of his nose. He turns. "Sean?" He swipes off his glasses and gets a look at me. "Are you okay? Is everything alright?"

The concern in his voice. The care in his eyes.

I smile. "It is, now."

He doesn't seem to read too much into that. "Did you go to the bonfire?"

I nod. "Sure did."

"Great. Made some new friends?"

"I don't remember any of their names."

He chuckles. "Well, at least you're getting around and meeting more people on the island."

"Did you handle the emergency at the bar?"

He stares at me, completely lost for a moment. "Oh." He laughs it off suddenly. "That. It wasn't an emergency. It was just … an overreaction. Chase has a tendency to, uh … to overreact. I wasn't actually needed."

The amazing and terrible thing about my ability to read people is it never shuts off. I feel the tension in his voice. "Why do I get the feeling you're pushing me away?"

His smile drops. "What? I'm not."

"Did you use the bar as an excuse to let me be on my own? Is that what really happened?"

"Sean ..."

"Just tell me what's going on."

He deflates. "Let's be real with each other here, okay? Things between us ... It got very intense, very quickly. We have only known each other for a few days. I put a roof over your head. However long you want that roof is up to you. I don't want you to feel obligated to me just because I'm the guy who gave you a hand. There are many men your age on this island."

"So? Do you like me or not?"

That causes him to finally look me in the eye. "What kind of question is that?"

"A simple one. Give me a simple answer. Do you like me or not?"

"I ..." His voice softens. "Whether or not I like you is not the point I'm trying to make here, Sean."

"Then what is the point?"

He leans forward with his elbows on his knees, head hanging. After a moment, he decides to tell me something else entirely. "Someone ... came to the bar tonight."

My heart jumps. "Someone ...?"

"Someone from my past."

For an unsettling second, I thought it was Ice. "Who?"

"I ... hesitate to call him an ex. I'm not sure what to call him. He was your age when I knew him. He had needs, too, but ... they were nothing like yours." His face tightens up, turning dark and heavy. "He had a need to *win* me. He saw me as a conquest. He pursued me to prove himself to his friends he came here with, to score the local bartender, to become the coveted hot new shit of Dreamwood Isle. What he called 'love', it was like a game of throwing darts to him. My heart was the bullseye. It was ten years ago."

"Ten years?"

"Seems like yesterday, the way the years fly by." Coop looks off, appearing bitter. "After he left me, I told all my friends he was just going back home. I told them it was the most beautiful summer I ever had. I painted this fairytale picture to them of how our love just happened at the wrong time. I ... was too ashamed to admit I got played by some fucking teenager." He shakes his head. "His kind of game, it was an efficient one. It gutted me like a fish, from one end to the other, leaving nothing. It's the reason I am the way I am. On one hand, I like taking care of ..." He shuts his eyes. "I like taking care of people. But I also need to protect my heart, what's left of it. I'm at constant war with myself. I feel like if I ever dare to let someone in ..."

I cross the room and stop right in front of him, so close he has to look up at me. "Let me say a few things, Coop."

His eyes are so small when he stares up at me, like I'm

the adult now and he's the lost boy. "Okay."

"I know what you're trying to tell me. The guy showed up. You're thinking things. You know I'm not him, but it's so easy to listen to the fear in your heart instead of the guy right in front of you, the guy who's saying he's *met* all of these guys my age on this island. You think I should spend time with them instead of you. To have fun with them. Go out with them. But you said it yourself: my needs are *not* like theirs. Not like this dart-throwing dick from your past. Cooper, you don't know what I want—what I *really* want. You think you're holding me back or … or depriving me somehow … or keeping me all to yourself. Like you, I've met hundreds of men out there, men who play games, men who have *needs*, men who lie. You are *nothing* like them."

I bring my hand to the back of Cooper's head, gently cradling it. His lips part. His eyes never leave mine.

"Cooper … I want to keep my promise to you, but you have to keep mine, too. To keep both our doors wide open to the possibility of anything." My heart swells as all of my words come out. "I don't want to keep wandering aimlessly. I'm tired of being afraid. If what we have is just a spark, and all we're destined to be is a stray and the man who took him in … so be it. But we won't know that after just one weekend. We need time. I want as much of it as you'll give me. I want to stay here as long as you'll have me. I want to make a life here."

Cooper rises from the chair right then. He brings a pair of fingers to my forehead, brushing away bangs. He seems deep in thought. "Doors wide open," he finally says.

"Doors wide open," I agree. "To anything. And if that dart-thrower comes back to your bar, you tell me."

"Sean ..."

"I've learned things out there, how to deal with guys, how to deal with liars and cheats like him."

"He won't be coming back. He wanted me to go to his room at the Sunnyview to chat ... but I didn't. I told him to leave my bar, and he left, and he won't come back."

I slide my hands around his waist, pulling him against me. "About time someone protects you, too, Coop. Maybe I'm not the only one who needed saving."

He gazes into my eyes, appearing sensitive and soft.

Is this what he looks like with all of his walls down? Have I finally found the real Cooper?

"Only time will tell if this can work," I say. "If there's something here. Something real."

After another moment of stargazing through my eyes, Cooper leans forward and puts a kiss on my forehead, then smiles at me. "Here's to looking after each other's hearts."

Bathed in lamplight with the wind beating fiercely against the window, we hold each other. I feel safe within his arms—wanted, hopeful, and safe.

I hope he feels the same way in mine.

CHAPTER 15

A SINGLE MONTH CAN REALLY CHANGE A PERSON.

Honestly, I had my doubts about this working out, ever since that night we held each other in an embrace that felt like it could last forever. The final week of Pride. The night Drake slipped into and ran out of my life for the last time. The day I was certain I'd be bidding farewell to Sean.

And now a month later, he's still under my roof.

Nagging me. Teasing me. Needing me.

Loving me.

And I wouldn't have it any other way.

"Are we doing dinner tonight?" I ask him.

We're sitting on the porch facing the water where we just enjoyed breakfast in the company of my plants and the crashing morning waves. He takes a sip of his orange juice and smiles. His face has filled out more. His skin is healthy and shiny from the sun. His eyes are bright and relaxed, too. Whenever he smiles, I see no hint of distress. He is at his most peaceful, his most inspired, his happiest.

"We can do Desert Moon again," I suggest. "Or even try something new on the mainland. There's that restaurant that just opened up near campus."

"Last night was amazing," Sean admits. "I didn't think I'd like oysters. They always looked gross to me."

"Life in a beach town, you're doomed to try every kind of seafood. Maybe I can finally convince you to try squid."

"It's bad enough eating something with no face. Now you want me to eat something with nineteen arms?"

"Actually, squid have eight arms and two tentacles, if we're being nitpicky."

Sean sighs. "And now you're gonna give me a lecture about the difference between an arm and a tentacle?"

"Nope. You can wonder about it all day long or google it, doesn't matter to me. I'm still wondering whether we're doing dinner tonight, like I asked."

He gulps the last of his juice, then sets down his glass. Something seems to occur to him. "Oh, I think I have a late modeling thing at the college. I need to ask Vann about it. I can't remember if it's tonight or tomorrow. He was going to take me so you wouldn't have to."

"I don't mind," I insist, leaning forward. "I'd be happy to drive you out to campus. Between our new bartender and Chase, the Easy Breezy's covered."

"Are you kidding me? This weekend is going to be just as busy as last weekend, if not worse. Everyone's getting in their last vacations before the summer's over. I'll take you up on your offer in the fall," he decides with a nod, "since it'll be calmer here on the island, and there will be twice as many classes going on, so I'll be busier and more needed."

He even sounds more confident than before, making all of these decisions, being proactive with his new life … It's a wonder I had doubts at all of Sean holding his own. I feel like I should just sit back, smile, and let him run things.

Isn't this exactly what I wanted for him?

"What?" he says, frowning.

I lift my eyebrows. "Hmm?"

"You're smiling. Why are you smiling?"

I'm just proud of you, I'd say, but instead I shrug. "It sounds to me like you have everything thought out."

"You think I'm wrong?"

"Nope. You're right. The bar will be busy tonight. I'll stick around in case the new bartender needs help or Chase has a panic attack over another nightmare Tinder date."

"He should stop using dating apps."

175

"Chase is convinced he's always one date away from paradise." I meet Sean's eyes. "You'll be back late, then?"

"Shouldn't be later than ten or eleven, if it's tonight."

"Still early enough for dessert on the boardwalk."

To that, he smiles. "Sounds great."

We gaze at each other, smiling at the idea, at ourselves, at whatever is happening between us.

Then, as usual, reality sets in.

Sean's eyes are as immediately present as they are so far away, like a reflection in the water I can't touch without the ripples stealing it away, or a dream I just woke up from and struggle to remember.

I wonder what we *are* becoming, if anything.

That night, I'm still lost in the same thought as I make drink after drink, absentmindedly staring off between the orders. Sean was right: it's a busy-as-hell Friday with no end in sight. Once one group clears out, another group is at the door to take their place. The bar is so packed and loud, it's anything but easy or breezy. I find myself checking the clock every ten minutes, wondering how Sean is doing. I try to picture him doing his modeling work, wondering what that must be like. Vann is with him, so I know Sean's safe and not being taken advantage of right now. They're all art students with legitimate goals and intentions. When he comes back, I get to hear all about the experience. Sean never holds back with me, wanting to share everything.

I wonder if I could have done modeling back in my twenties. I'm not sure I have the daringness to do it. I'd be too stiff in front of the camera or too impatient to hold a pose for a room of painters or meticulous illustrators. Sean has found more than just a place for himself; he's found a life full of friends, contacts, and purpose.

"So have you fellas used the L word yet?"

Chase asks me this during the rush when we're both behind the counter. I'm in the middle of making shots.

"Nope."

"Really? You guys have gotten so close, though."

I give him a look. "How do you know how close we've gotten? The last time Sean helped out here was nearly three weeks ago and you didn't even notice him."

"He works like a ninja!"

"Are you spying on me, Chase?" I tease him. "Peeking through my bedroom window?"

He gives me side-eye. "What would I see if I did?"

I give him side-eye right back. "Get back to ringing up your customers before you forget to charge them at all, you dirty perv."

"That only happened *once* because the guy was *cute*," groans Chase, "and I am *not* a dirty perv. I'm a very *clean* perv." He puffs up his chest, appearing proud of his joke.

The truth is, his question *chases* me around all night— pun intended. I never expected to truly fall into a serious, committed relationship with Sean. Ever since that night of his first bonfire—where I waited anxiously at home after having an unexpected blast from the past at the bar—the two of us seemed to have settled into something of a nice and comfortable roommates-with-benefits situation.

The benefits are interpretive at best. Cuddling at night. Kissing without reservation. Sean occasional strutting out of the shower wearing nothing at all, like irresistible bait at the end of a hook, knowing I'm doomed to bite.

And I take him out on the town now and then. We grab lunch and dinner when his new friends aren't treating him. We went to a movie last week and even ran into Adrian's brother Skipper, who is a year younger than Sean, as he was skateboarding by.

It's always a thought in the back of my head, no matter what we're doing together. What are we, exactly? What is going to come out of this arrangement, if anything at all?

Sean said time would tell.

I agreed with him and left my door open.

Life keeps changing—yet staying exactly the same.

"So tell me, has the honeymoon phase ended already?"

It's Chase again about half an hour later. This time he's caught me back in the stockroom. "What?"

"The honeymoon phase. You and Sean. Is it over?"

"Never really started, I think. Why is your nose so far up in my business, anyway?"

Chase lifts his hands innocently. "Just asking!"

"And you won't *stop* asking," I point out.

"Look, my life is kind of … lonesome lately, alright? I come to the bar. I go home to my cat. And when I'm not at either place, I'm surfing on Sugarberry Beach. And when I'm not doing that, I'm wondering why Finn hasn't called me to hang out all summer, then remember he's way busy with all his responsibilities and doesn't have time for friendships anymore. Then I wonder what I'm doing with my own life, as well as who I'm doing it with, and I feel like a failure. Boss, what I'm trying to say is whenever I see you guys together, it gives me hope. You were like me. Now you've got Sean. I just want to know if you're happy."

I stare at Chase, dumbfounded.

Upon seeing the look I'm making, he fights a blush. "I think I'll … uh, sorry. I'll go back onto the floor." He hides his face and slips out of the stockroom.

Am I happy?

It's a legitimate question.

I don't blame Chase for asking any more than I blame myself for not knowing the answer.

And that's not even addressing this L word situation.

I feel like I'm in high school again, stressing over some unread love letter I slipped in my crush's locker. Honestly, this is kind of sad.

It's also fucking fun.

179

Sean keeps me feeling young. He gives me hope that my best days aren't behind me, but rather yet to come. He keeps me wondering. I can't predict what will happen each day that goes by, and I love it that way. Life has never felt more fresh and full of possibilities.

So why can't I answer that basic question?

Are you happy?

Business slows as the night carries on, and soon, just a few of the island regulars occupy the bar when I step onto the front steps for some air. The light from the Quicksilver Strand spill onto the beach, though all the restaurants are closed at this hour, only a few workers remaining to carry out their closing duties. I come around to the side of the building and lean against a lamppost, watching Boardwalk Street. A car goes past. Then a trio of guys who sound (and look) like they just hit up El Amado, the nightclub. Three more cars, all headed to the north end of the island. I make a game of it and start counting the cars, gnawing on my lip and resisting the temptation to torture myself further with thoughts, worries, and unanswered questions.

Crunching in the dirt draws my attention. It's Adrian approaching from the boardwalk with a small white box in his hand bearing the Thalassa logo. "Guess your guy hasn't shown up yet?"

"Just a little late is all." I take the box from Adrian and nod. "Thanks for the hookup."

"Oh, it's not a freebie. You owe me a drink some night this week. I'm gonna need it."

"I bet you will." I weigh the box in my hand, then find my mind wandering. "Are you happy, Adrian?"

He looks at me. "Happy?"

"It was just a couple months ago that you were the hot bachelor on the island like you've always been, with a new piece of candy in your bed every weekend. Now you have a man in your life … a man you truly love." I look at him. "So are you happy?"

"Of course I'm happy. Why wouldn't I be?"

"How long did it take before you used the L word?"

He stares at me like I've lost my mind.

Maybe I have. "Never mind. I'm overthinking. Thanks again for this," I say with a lift of the box. "We would have been there to eat this in person, but I guess he had more to do on campus than he anticipated. Still waiting on Vann's car to pop around the corner."

"Vann? Ooh, better be careful with that one." Adrian lets out a laugh. "The guy is like a snake charmer."

I quirk an eyebrow. "Snake charmer?"

"I know he and Toby haven't been here all that long, but the love of my life admitted to once having a thing for Vann. I almost lost my man to Vann's tortured artist charm. Thankfully, I'm slightly *more* charming."

I frown. "Hmm."

He notices. "Oh, don't worry. I'm mostly kidding."

"'Mostly kidding' …?"

"Yeah, he won't take Sean away from you. Why would you even think that? He's got Toby. I just meant … well, you know how those artist types are. Full of dark passion, inspiring each other, baring their souls …" He looks at me. "Am I making this better or worse?"

I don't answer, keeping my hardened eyes on the road.

"Oh, and he doesn't have a car." Adrian leans into my ear. "Vann rides a—"

Just then, the roar of a motorcycle cracks through the air like a monster, shaking me fully awake. Up the road comes a motorcycle, which swiftly hops onto the dirt with a growl, then stops some distance from us. Vann, noticing me, nods my way and gives a short wave.

That's when I notice his passenger is clinging to him from behind—my Sean.

My grip on the little white box tightens.

Sean hops off the bike, pulls off his helmet, and hands it back to Vann. "Thanks so much. I'll see you tomorrow!" To that, Vann nods, gives me another wave, then lets his engine rip as he soars away, disappearing around the corner.

Sean, all smiles and looking like he's walking on air, comes up to me. "Hey there, Coop! Adrian," he says with a nod, noticing him.

Adrian snorts. "Can that bike be any louder?"

"You think *that's* loud? Should've heard him burning rubber down the causeway. I could barely feel my face." Sean's eyes drop to the box in my hand. "What's that?"

"Dessert," I answer.

"Oh." He puts a hand to his mouth, then winces. "I'm sorry. I lost track of time. I … I forgot we had plans."

"They weren't official." I put on a smile. "It's alright."

"No, no, it isn't."

"I said it's alright. I was caught up at the bar, anyway."

"Really? You sure?"

That was a lie. I could've left hours ago. "Yep. No big deal." I give Adrian a pat on the back. "Thanks for the nice treat, my friend. I guess we'll be off."

Adrian, who is apparently still wondering whether or not his whole rant about Vann's irresistible dark charm just destroyed my self-confidence, gives an absent nod. "Sure. I am happy to, uh, help out."

I'm sure you are, Adrian.

Sean and I don't make it back home. Sitting in my car in the back parking lot of the bar, we pop open the box and dig right in with a pair of wrapped plastic forks I had in my glove box. I don't think this is the elegant way the chefs at Thalassa intended their delicacy to be enjoyed, but neither I nor Sean care. Every bite is just as sweet.

It's triple chocolate melting fudge cake, by the way.

"*Fuck* me," groans Sean for the sixth or seventh time.

I smile back at him, chewing. "I know, right?"

"I mean, just, like ... *fuck* me, this is good."

We're both holding the box over my center console as we trade bites. "You know, if you're gonna go all pro with your newfound modeling career ..."

"Nah, it's just a thing for now."

"... and taking on these amazing late-night—"

"Wait." Sean eyes me. "Are you about to bodyshame me out of eating this dessert?"

"What? No, not at all. Eat your heart out."

"Because I know I gotta keep in shape," he goes on. "It doesn't mean I can't indulge now and then. I'm not gonna be a runway model or something. I don't have the height."

People have been talking to him at the school. I hear their words coming out of his mouth, giving him ideas and nixing others. "That wasn't where I was going."

"So what is it?" asks Sean.

I nod at the glove box. "There was more than just these forks in there."

He frowns, his chewing stopped. He stabs his fork into the cake and goes for the glove box again. That's when he sees the thin present, wrapped in shiny blue paper with a ribbon. "It isn't my birthday," he says, mouth full.

"Don't need an occasion to wrap a gift for you."

He swallows his bite. "Can I open it?"

"Of course."

He tears off the wrapping paper and ribbon with such speed and urgency, I lift my eyebrows in surprise. When the paper falls off, his eyes go big.

"You got me a phone?" He looks at me, shocked. "You got me a—a—This is expensive, Coop."

"Don't worry about it. Like I was trying to explain, if you're planning to go all pro with your modeling gigs, you will need a way to gather your contacts that doesn't involve all this word-of-mouth through Toby or Vann. I want you to be able to take even more charge of your life."

"I will pay you back," he states, still staring at the box. He hasn't even opened it yet to look at the actual phone.

"I know you said your original phone was stolen back in San Antonio. It's been an idea on my mind for the past couple weeks now, wanting to get you your own phone."

"Hey, I can text you if I'm gonna be late again. And … And you can text me, too. Now incidents like tonight won't happen again."

"Sure, that too."

He turns to me. "I don't know how to thank you, Coop. I wasn't expecting this. Not even a little bit."

The sweet and adoring look in Sean's eyes right now is payment enough. "You deserve to have it, Sean. I love you. And I want to take care of—"

My throat closes.

What did I just say?

The car is pierced by a terrifying silence.

Then Sean smiles back, leans over the center console, and kisses me. When he pulls away, our eyes lock on each other's. He looks on the verge of tears. I can't blink.

I feel a world of unspoken emotion passing between us right now.

Did I say the right thing?

Will all of my fears die a quick death in this car?

Are my unanswered questions at last going to find their answers?

In the dreadful silence, he finally parts his lips to reply.

He says: "Thank you so much, Coop."

I continue staring at him.

Staring and staring and staring.

And staring some more.

Then: "O-Of course," I choke back in reply.

He settles back into his seat with a manic chuckle. "I can't believe it. You really did catch me by surprise, Coop. I thought sharing a midnight dessert from an upscale place in your car was the big special plan. Wow ..." He stuffs his mouth with another bite of fudgy cake.

I smile blankly back at him, glass-eyed, frozen.

He didn't say it back.

CHAPTER 16

SEANY

HONESTLY, I'M FEELING GREAT ABOUT EVERYTHING.

My living situation. My new career. The friends I made in Toby, Vann, and my regulars at the college. Now and then helping out at the bar. Everything feels like some kind of perfect design falling into place.

A design I never dreamed I'd ever call my own.

It's Saturday morning, one of the last weekends of the summer, and as I gaze at Vann's artwork—now hanging in Cooper's living room—I can't seem to believe the life I'm living. I'm not a movie star. I'm not taking baths in cash. I'm simply well-adjusted for the first time in years.

I'm happy.

Ding! My phone chimes at me. It's such a new sound, it startles me every time. I can't believe I have a phone that can chime at me again.

VANN

Got another gig for you tonight. You
OK with taking off your shirt?

I grin down at the message and tell him that's fine with me. When he replies with a thumbs-up and tells me he'll pick me up later, I pocket my phone. Whistling to myself, I head out the door and lock up behind me. Under a bright blue sky with the sun shining overhead, I pop on my shades and stroll down the street.

I feel like king of the island.

"Nope, that's cheating," states Mars.

"It's not!" cries Toby through his laughter. "Perfectly legitimate special moves are *not* cheating."

"Looks like cheating to me."

"Call it what you want, I'm still winning."

Mars and Toby always bicker like brother and sister at the arcade. When it's my turn, I jump into the game, taking over for Toby, and Mars finally scores her first win in the past hour. No one stands a chance against *gamer god Toby*, so when Mars and I play each other, it feels like a leveled playing field.

"What time does Vann come back?" asks Mars while the three of us cool off at the Desert Moon Diner, finished with gaming for the afternoon.

"Late tonight, I think," answers Toby, "but I think he's swinging by to pick up Sean here for a thing."

"Always picking up Sean for a thing," sings Mars. She eyes me. "You've had a lot going on lately, huh?"

My mouth is full of chips and salsa. "Yep," I mumble through my mouthful.

"Hope you're getting paid well enough."

"Yeah, of course." I swallow my bite, then nudge Toby. "You ever pose for your boyfriend's art? He just said the gig tonight requires me taking my shirt off."

"Not intentionally," admits Toby after a sip of his soda. "I'll be relaxing in a chair on my phone or something, and I catch Vann with his sketchpad drawing me from across the room. He's never not working."

"Oh, you artists," sings Mars with a sigh, crossing her arms on the table to lay her head down. "What a life."

Toby chuckles. "What do you mean?"

"I'm terrible at drawing stuff," she says. "I don't even know how you begin."

"Well, it's simple. You just have to look at something with enough honesty to see its essence. Then you put that onto paper in a creative way. I think it's why Vann draws demons and monsters all the time. He likes to think we're all hiding a demon inside of us, and the more we suppress it, the more good we seem."

Mars lifts her head and makes a face. "So we're all, like, inherently evil or something?"

"Not really. Maybe more inherently playful. Inherently childlike and impulsive and yearning for chaos." Toby puts more salsa onto his plate, then frowns. "Hmm, it does … kinda sound evil, thinking of it that way."

"What do you think, Seany?" asks Mars. "Oops, sorry, I meant *Sean*. Old habit."

I was in the middle of picking out my next tortilla chip when she asks. I snatch the perfect one, then thoughtfully gaze at it as I consider my answer. "I think about all of the different people I've met out there. What they want. What they're willing to do to get it. Whether they're inherently good or bad people." I frown. "I've seen what desperation does to good people. I mean, people always want to insist they're good and honest, but if you put anyone in a terrible enough situation, you'd be surprised what they're willing to do to survive."

Mars winces. "So you think we're all evil inside?"

I stare at the chip for a long time.

Toby puts a hand on my back. "It's okay, Sean. It's all just hypothetical fun. Don't need to think too much about it. Maybe Vann just draws demons because they're cool."

I look up at him, shaken out of my thoughts, and smile.

I'm still thinking about demons and good and evil after Vann picks me up to take me to the gig. I'm thinking about it after taking off my shirt and posing for the camera. Each time the camera flashes, I feel like a different demon in one of Vann's twisted, beautiful art pieces.

It's a weird feeling. To be so happy with my life.

And yet with every happy day I have, there are a dozen of unhappy days that had to pass to get me here. Days of fear. Days of hunger. Days where I would have considered doing terrible things to survive. And days where I watched others do terrible things.

There might live a little demon inside each of us.

A demon that Vann loves to turn into art, to bring out onto the canvas, to expose for the world.

But I'm determined now more than ever to be stronger than the demon inside me. I must commit to my beautiful life with Cooper and take hold of and enjoy as many good days as I can. Eventually, I want to proudly say I have got more beautiful days in my life than bad ones. Beautiful days like today, where I didn't have a care in the world except hanging out at the arcade with friends, stuffing my face with chips and salsa at Desert Moon Diner, and riding the back of Vann's motorcycle to work a modeling gig.

And beautiful nights where I come home to Cooper.

The moment Vann drops me off at home, I find Coop standing there ready to greet me. "Did you have fun?"

I rush up to him and let his arms wrap around me. My safe space. My protector. My warmth.

He chuckles warmly. "I take that as a yes."

I peer up into his eyes. "Tonight's a movie night."

"Oh, is it?" He strokes my hair. "What kind of movie? You pick."

"You always make me pick."

"Because you always pick the best movies."

I bite my lip. My heart flutters happily. I grab hold of his waist and pull him against me for a kiss. His breath is warm against my face. I feel his grip tightening around me as our kiss deepens. Then my hands slide down his back to take two meaty handfuls of his ass. He does the same, and his hands grip me so tightly, I feel my cheeks spread as he lifts me up off the ground. He takes me to his bedroom and places me on the bed like a prince, before then peeling off my clothes like they're in the way, piece by piece, until not even a sock remains.

I never pick a movie.

We never make it to watching one at all.

An hour and a half later, we're naked and sweaty. Our bodies are sprawled out on his bed, clothes scattered all over the floor, and from his window whistles the sweetest night breeze from off the beach.

"There's only one thing that could've made today even more perfect," I murmur as we enjoy our afterglow.

"Mmm, and what's that?"

"Having you there for every moment of it."

I feel the bed shake from his light chuckling. "You just want to laugh at how *bad* I am at arcade games."

"We also ate at Desert Moon."

"Mmm … Taqueria Tía Juanitas is better."

"You're only saying that out of loyalty to Mars's mom. Mars was with us, by the way."

"*Traitor*," growls Cooper playfully.

"I just had so much fun today." I can't wipe the smile off of my face. "I know you had to do things at the bar. We have our lives apart, and we have our lives together. It's all a beautiful design."

"Hmm. 'A beautiful design' … That sounds nice." He runs his fingers gently through my hair. "You're beautiful, you know that, Sean? Inside and out."

Inside and out.

I smile as he strokes my hair, wondering about beauty. The way it looks. The way it seems. The way it really is.

Demons can be beautiful, too.

But does that make them good?

As we fall asleep together sometime later, I find myself wondering about a certain night in his car over fudgy cake from Thalassa when he let slip a word from his lips.

The "love" word.

He heard it. I heard it.

Yet all I did was kiss him and say nothing.

Why didn't I say it back?

Why did my ears seem to reject it the moment they were given such a beautiful gift?

As I lie here in his arms at the end of a perfect day, I'm left thinking more about demons and less of good things. I try to keep smiling, but I can't help feel like an imposter in this life I don't deserve.

I feel the claws of my past, like an ugly creature with no morals, digging its way out of my chest, desperate to reclaim me again. The creature that was fed with all of my father's worst words and drinking benders. The creature who learned how to survive on the streets at night. It grins as it assesses my new, beautiful life, wondering how it can ruin this perfect thing I now have and cherish.

I have a history of losing things I love.

Everything I cherish goes away eventually.

That creature reminds me I don't deserve this life. I did not earn this life. A picture of this creature now hangs on Cooper's wall, like a dark reminder of who I really am— this creature, who whispers in my ear that this life is just another can of nuts I'm greedily prying out of Cooper's good and loving hands.

CHAPTER 17

COOPER

THE BONFIRE GLOWS BRIGHTLY AGAINST THE NIGHT SKY.

All around, friendly faces and laughter. Beer. Drunken banter. One guy strumming a guitar and singing badly. The stars fill the horizon, my heart is as warm as that fire before my eyes, and I'm not sure there's a damned thing anyone could do to make this night any better.

"About time we see your ass at one of these," mutters Adrian with a beer in his hand.

I shrug. "Sean basically dragged me. He's out there in the crowd somewhere with his friends, if he's not up at your mom's house with Skipper and the others."

"I don't know. I'm not their babysitter." Adrian kicks his drink back.

I smirk. "Babysitter?"

He grins. "I gotta get a jab in whenever I can. It's too much fun, seeing an old man like you kicking it hard with someone who's younger than me." He squints into the fire. "Though, to be honest, there's something special with that Sean, even I gotta admit. He's *seen* stuff, y'know? You ... You can just tell by looking at him. He's *seen* stuff."

I stare at the fire myself. "Yeah," I say after a while, nodding slowly. "But he's coming around. Bit by bit. He's seeing what life can be like when things are good. I think we all deserve that chance."

"Mm-hmm."

I eye Adrian. "So where's your man, huh? I thought he was coming tonight."

"He is. He's with Kent and Jonah to get more beer or something. Hey, have you seen Finn? He was supposed to be here too, but I think he's fighting with his boyfriend."

"Again?"

"There's something up with those guys. Their energy is all over the place."

I shrug. "Finn's energy is always all over the place. He overworks himself at the fair. His dad keeps loading new responsibilities onto his back. Finn will be burnt out before he's twenty-five, I swear."

"Poor guy." He glances at me. "Things don't seem to be anywhere near fizzling out with you and lover boy."

I'm still scanning the crowd, wondering where Sean is. Maybe he really is up at Adrian's mom's house, which is one of these houses by the beach, quite a bit of ways down from mine. "Yeah, they're pretty strong."

"You guys seem to be a serious thing."

I look at him. "You seem surprised."

He shrugs. "If I'm being honest, yeah, a bit. I thought Sean might be … like … a pet project or something."

"A 'pet project' …? The fuck?"

"Nothing bad. I just thought once you helped get him back on his feet, he might be someone you someday usher off to find his own life. I guess part of me didn't expect the guy to actually find a life here … with you."

"Huh."

"Listen, Coop, I know you look at me as some horny animal who doesn't know anything, but I learned a lot this summer, and I recognize that lost look in your eyes."

"Really?"

"Yep. Now answer this: How do you feel about him?"

The question rings like a bell in my ears. Despite all the noise on the beach, the only thing I hear is the crackling of the bonfire and Adrian's hard words.

"I care deeply for him," I answer.

"Obviously. And?"

"And I ..." My eyes wander. "I feel ..." Breath escapes my lips in a doleful sigh. "I feel like I love him in a ... in a different way. A natural way."

"What do you mean?"

"It isn't the crazy, exotic kind of love that has me just wanting to have sex with him. It's a love that transcends all of that. I want to see him succeed. I want to see him happy. I want to help him realize his goals and find a future he can believe in. Something real and pure and true."

"That sounds pretty serious, man."

"But it's even more than that." I take a step toward the fire as it dances before my eyes. "Sean gives me a sense of purpose again. When I'm with him, I feel like my existence *matters*. I'm showing myself that I am capable of bringing goodness into this world because I'm able to give Sean the chance to bring *his* goodness into the world."

Adrian faces me and slaps a hand on my back. "Look, if you're feeling this deeply about this guy, then you need to go all in. Commit to him. To Sean. That was the biggest mistake I almost made with my life, letting it slip on by and committing to nothing. Don't be me. Commit to him."

I stare at Adrian again, overcome.

Commit to him. Commit to Sean.

Why do those words terrify me?

I reconnect with Sean sometime later when the bonfire starts calming down and people begin heading home. After running off with Mars and the others, he came back with a whole ton of stories he wanted to share with me. I barely catch any of it as he excitedly shares everything with me, too preoccupied with my own thoughts. He reminds me so much of myself when I was his age, overly excited about anything, laughing too much, amazed by the tiniest things.

All of those possibilities that live in his eyes of what his life could be, I could be stealing them away if I commit to Sean. When I told him I loved him. If I expected to hear it back. It's like caging a bird the moment I just set it free.

How can I look at it any other way?

Why would I want to do that to Sean, just when he is in the middle of realizing how amazing and limitless his life could be now?

"Two large popcorns please," he says at the counter. "And a large blue raspberry slushy. And a—oh, Coop, do you like Sweetarts? I like Sweetarts. Okay, add one of those, please."

We catch a midnight movie at the theater because Sean is riding a crazy kind of high tonight, and after our time at the bonfire, neither of us seem settled enough to sleep. In the back row, we feast on popcorn, candy, and slushies as a low-budget fantasy movie from the 90s plays on the screen. Besides us, there are only two others in the whole theater, and they're all the way in the front row, so Sean doesn't hold back in talking through the entire feature. He can't sit still. He tells me about something hilarious Mars said. He tells me about a gig last week that felt weird at first, but got more comfortable as the shoot went on. He tells me how he heard stories about Toby and Vann's senior year and how it made him wonder how his own would have went, if he had the chance to finish it. "But I think I should really consider getting a GED," he decides between handfuls of popcorn. "It's unlikely I'm going back. And with my life here, I may want to pursue more things in my future. School's behind me now. The rest of my life is ahead."

It's almost as if Sean himself is warning me not to get too attached. He's a professional runner with a long road ahead of him, and he's finally getting his running shoes on.

This was my plan all along, wasn't it?

To help him. To give him a roof, security, and a chance to succeed. To feed him, clothe him, and take care of him.

To give him what the world refused to give him.

A fair shot.

"Are you gonna eat any of your Sweetarts? You didn't even open yours yet and look at me, I'm already down to my last handful."

So I should be happy about what I've done for him.

"They're all yours," I say with a smile.

"Hmm." He snuggles up against my side, since the armrest between us has been shoved away, then tears open the bag. "How about I eat one, then feed you one?"

"As long as you don't feed me the yellow ones."

"Which one's your favorite, then?"

"Reds."

"I'll remember that," says Sean as he fishes a red one out, then pokes it at my lips. "Open up, baby."

I gaze at him. "'Baby'? *You're* calling *me* ba—?" He pops it into my mouth before I can finish the word. I chew on it as I smirk. "Sweet."

"And tart. Hence the name. Want another, baby?"

"Is this a new thing we're starting? 'Baby'?"

"Sure. I'm feeling playful tonight." He grins at me. His eyes practically sparkle in the bright light coming off the big screen. "If you don't like 'baby', I can call you *Coopy*."

I snort. "Oh, no you don't, boy. You are *not* bringing back Coopy or else I'm bringing back Seany."

He laughs and twists around to rest his head in my lap, then stares up at me. His smile fades as his big bright eyes search mine. "Sean ... Seany ... I sometimes wonder if they're two different people now. One is the demon inside of me who has seen and done terrible things. The other ..." He shrugs. "The other one is who I want to be. One's a red candy ... the other, yellow. One is baby ... the other, not."

I bring my hand to his hair and gently stroke, watching his face with concern. "What do you mean?"

"You told me about your past self. Long before you and I met. Your crazy, promiscuous twenties. Your days of

201

partying and living it up." He tilts his head as he gazes up into my eyes. "Do you ever think of the Young Coop?— your own *Coopy*?"

"From time to time, I guess. What about him?"

"Do you ever wish he was around again? Do you ever get the, like, *hankering* to be a crazy, fun-for-all party boy again, doing whatever you want, setting the clubs on fire?"

The idea almost makes me laugh. "Not anymore."

"So what's your secret? How did you cut ties with that younger you? How did you … tame your own demon?"

"I've lived many more years than you. Time did most of the work." Sean feeds me another red one by surprise, then chuckles at the look on my face. I gaze down at him. "I think the circumstances of my life changed. Suddenly I wasn't able to be that version of myself anymore. I needed to be something else. It was time to grow up."

"To grow up. Hmm …" There's a loud sound from the movie, causing him to lift his head and look at the screen for a moment. I watch the movie flickering over his eyes.

I keep caressing his soft, messy hair. "Are you worried about your own past self? Is that why you're asking about how I dealt with mine?"

"I try not to think about it. But it's not easy."

"If it means anything to you, I think you've grown up quite a bit these past few weeks."

He faces me again. "Really?"

"These are *your* new circumstances. Your friends. This island. All the great stuff you've got going on." I smile. "I think in time, you won't even remember your old pain. It'll all be memories. Behind you. Far, far away … Nowhere it can hurt you or touch you ever again."

With his head in my lap gazing up at me, his eyes look like bottomless pools of emotion. I could lean too far into them and fall forever.

"You promise?" he says quietly.

I caress his face. "Yeah, baby. I promise."

He lifts himself up to kiss me. The kiss isn't short. It feels deep, loving, and meaningful. It casts away every fear in our minds. It finishes every thought we had and didn't voice. It takes care of all our worries and leaves us feeling free, connected, and safe.

Then he pulls away and peers into my eyes. "So *I'm* the baby, then?"

I laugh. "Feed me another red and we'll find out."

He does just that, then cuddles against me with the rest of the bag in hand as we resume watching the movie. I tuck him under an arm and hold him close, enjoying every bit of time we've got together.

It's almost two in the morning when the movie's over. Sean still looks like he's got enough energy to last an entire marathon, which may very well happen when we get home, provided I don't pass out immediately. We throw away our trash, bid farewell to the sleepy-eyed usher waiting on us to leave, then make our way out of the theater.

As we cross the parking lot, he takes hold of my hand. I glance at him with a curious look, smile, then decide to let it happen, our hands swinging playfully between us. It feels like the most natural thing in the world—us walking side by side in our sweet little paradise.

When we reach the corner, however, Sean stops cold. He looks over his shoulder. Concerned, I follow his line of sight to a park across the street.

After a moment, I look back at Sean. "What's wrong?"

He keeps staring, completely silent, still, unblinking. "I thought I saw something," he finally chokes.

"Saw what?"

His eyes won't pull away from the park. I look again. I see no one there. Not even an animal, bird, or suspicious shadow. Just the usual trees, the old benches, the trashcans, and the small spread of concrete that once was a basketball court, but is now only used occasionally by skaters.

I look at him again. "Sean? Are you alright?"

He peels his eyes from the park at last and puts on a rather sudden smile. "I'm perfect. Let's go home ... *baby*."

I smile back as we continue walking. I can't help but glance one last time over my shoulder, wondering what it was that arrested Sean so deeply—if anything at all.

CHAPTER 18

SEANY

"NAILED IT."

I pull my tank undershirt back on over my head, then shrug. "I hope it turns out well."

"You're the most photogenic person I've literally ever met or worked with," says Lily, a photography student with straight black hair to her shoulders and thick red glasses. "Of course it'll turn out well, once I get around to editing these later tonight. Y'know what? I think you could charge even more than you do."

I blink. "Really? I thought I'm already charging a lot."

"Not even close. What do you think, SJ?"

Her gangly man-bunned roommate-slash-classmate SJ, who's been sitting on a stool in the back after helping set up the lighting at the start of the shoot, looks up from his phone. "Huh? Oh … y'mean how much he charges? Heh, yeah, he's selling himself short."

"See? Ask Vann, bet he'll tell you the same."

"I'm not a professional, though," I point out as I slip off the pants Lily gave me and put my own shorts back on. "And everyone on campus is already burdened enough—"

"With student loans and tuition? Sure, but we're all artists here. We know the value of compensating for time and work. We know 'exposure' doesn't pay bills. Fuck this 'do it for exposure' bullshit. The only *exposure* I will ever respect is the amount of light my baby's aperture lets in," she says, giving her camera a loving pat.

"Yeah, man, don't be too humble," says SJ as he stuffs things away in his backpack. "Charge more. It's your body you're giving up, anyway."

I pause, considering that for a moment as my flamingo button-up shirt hangs in my fist. I never saw it as "giving up my body". He makes it sound like something else.

Nevertheless, I find myself inspired by the idea of charging more. Aren't I worth it? Hell, my means of getting money since leaving home have been questionable and often involve thievery and deceit, it feels pretty amazing to earn honest money like this.

I'll be able to pay back Coop for my phone in no time.

When I step out of the cramped studio (it's actually a repurposed guest bedroom in Lily and SJ's apartment), I find Vann on the couch with his sketchpad, gnawing on his lip as he draws. He closes his pad and looks up at me. "All done? How'd it go? Did Lily get you naked yet?"

"Vann, please," mutters Lily. "That was just *once*, and it was my ex-girlfriend who modeled, and we broke up before I could even use our work in anything. It's for the best. We did some great work that day, and I'd be damned if I became famous on my ex's body. Goddess works in mysterious ways."

SJ is already out of the studio and in the kitchen. "You guys want anything before you head out? I'm thinking 'bout cooking up some chicken nugs."

"I would," says Vann, "but Toby's waiting for me back home. Maybe next time?"

"Wait. He is?" I turn to Vann. "You should've told me. Coop could have picked me up, or—"

"Nah, it's okay. Toby likes eating late, and I needed the time to work on *this*." He gives his sketchpad a swat of his hand. "Besides, he's been obsessed with a new game lately, so this gives him gaming time. In other words: valuable, precious, don't-you-dare-interrupt-me time."

"Oh ... I see." I stuff my hands down my pockets—and that's when I remember. I yank out my phone. "I totally forgot! I've got a phone now. I need to get your number before I go, Lily."

"Number?" She has joined SJ in the kitchen, fishing for something in a high-up cupboard. She peers over her shoulder at me. "Oh, that's new. No longer communicating through Vann? When'd you get a phone?"

"Week or so ago. Coop got it for me." I face the screen to both her and SJ, showing off my background image: a selfie of me and Coop sitting on his porch with the plants. "Nice view, right?"

"How cute," she sings. "Coop's that older guy you're living with, right?"

"Yep."

She smirks. "Daddy bought you a fancy phone, huh? Someone must've been a good boy," she says teasingly.

"I—What?" I retract my phone. "No, it's just—"

"Sounds like Sean-boy's got himself a sugar daddy," SJ pitches in with a nudge into Lily's ribs. "I wish I had someone spoiling me like that."

"I'm paying him back for it," I interject.

But they don't hear me. "I'm still rocking my same old phone from high school," mumbles Lily as she sets a pair of bowls on the counter. "I could use an upgrade."

"Dude, you should take advantage of that situationship while you're in it," says SJ, giving his unasked-for advice. "Get a nice wardrobe for your modeling gigs. Some bling,

208

maybe. Get him to set you up a modeling website. If you really work him good, maybe you can get a car out of it."

Lily cackles. "SJ, stop! You're so bad."

"Hey, just saying, it's what I'd do. Is this guy loaded?"

"Seriously, SJ!" But Lily herself can't stop laughing.

"Sean can take a little humor," SJ insists. "Besides, it's him who's taking off his clothes in front of cameras. Isn't he basically halfway to doing porn?"

"It isn't porn! What the hell?" cries Lily through her tears of laughter.

"Nah, I'm just playing. But really, you're lying if you say people won't get off lookin' at his hot pics. I popped a semi just watching you guys work and I'm straight." Lily keeps going back and forth between cackling and gasping. She can barely get a word in. "When you've got the looks, why not bank on them? Be the trophy boyfriend. Milk that lonely Coop guy for all he's worth. Hell, I'd do it if I didn't look like a wrung-out mop."

I stare at them as they continue to go back and forth like I'm not even here. I don't know when I do it, but I slip my phone back into my pocket, ashamed of it suddenly.

It's ten minutes later while walking through the dimly-lit parking lot in front of the dorms that Vann growls out the words, "I could've fucking killed him."

I blink. "What do you mean?"

"I am so sorry, Sean."

"For what?"

"I should've stood up for you in there. I should've said something. I should've—"

"Oh. No, no. Don't worry about it."

"Really, I should have. SJ is messed up and immature and terrible. I knew that already. He makes comments in class just to shock everyone. But I expected so much more from Lily other than standing by and laughing with him."

"It's okay," I assure Vann. "I guess I … told them a bit too much about my personal life. Cooper and all of that."

"So? That doesn't give them any right to—"

"And it's late. It's been a long day of shooting for both of them. I was their last model. I think they were just, like, tired and blowing off steam, being funny, whatever. Maybe they had a point." I shrug and hug myself as we walk. "I … I'm making money with my looks."

"Seriously, Sean? Don't even go there."

I look at Vann. "Are you mad at me?"

He stops. "You? No, Sean, I'm not mad at you. I'm … fucking *furious* those two even put these thoughts into your head, as if you're nothing more than a prostitute. What the hell is wrong with them?"

"They don't know my situation. It's fine."

"No, it's not." He sighs. "You're too forgiving, Sean. And I … I should have said something."

He resumes walking.

I follow.

We arrive at his bike after a while. He hands me the spare helmet, then puts on his own. It's while strapping on my helmet that I catch Vann sneaking a glance at me.

Actually, not me; the ugly boomerang scar on my arm.

"Knife wound," I say, answering his question.

He meets my eyes, caught. "Oh. Sorry."

"For staring? It's fine, no biggie. You've probably seen it before and wondered. If it helps, just assume everything went wrong one Thanksgiving when I was trying to carve a turkey for my sweet family and got myself this keepsake. It makes the scar cuter, when you make up a story." I resume strapping on my helmet.

Vann's frozen. "Really. I'm sorry for … not standing up for you in there. And for staring just now. I *have* noticed the scar and just … never asked."

"You don't have to be sorry for anything. It's just … a little scar from my past," I say with an inward smile.

He comes up to the bike, then stops, appearing to think for a moment. "Y'know … we all have pasts. Toby used to be pushed around by a cocky jock at school and his loser stepdad at home. I was kicked out of schools through my teen years and shuffled around the country by my image-obsessed parents. Our friend Kelsey used to live on the streets of a casino town by the beach before a gay couple in Spruce adopted her and brought her into all our lives. None of us can say what life is like in anyone else's shoes but our own." He faces me. "But we should still respect each other's scars just the same."

I peer at my scar, running a finger along it. Then I make a funny face. "Personally, I think it makes me look like a badass, and—"

"They shouldn't have talked about you and Cooper like that," says Vann, pressing on despite my effort at humor. "He's not your sugar daddy. He doesn't 'spoil' you. You are a model. And even if you *were* doing porn, so what? That's your business. Porn actors are people too." He huffs. "It was callous for them to say all that the way they did."

I drop my hand from the scar. "We get looked at, Coop and I. I know that. Few understand us. I don't even know if *we* understand us sometimes."

"Doesn't matter what anyone thinks."

"Thank you anyway, Vann. For being a friend."

He growls and peers back at the building. "I should go back in there and tell them that wasn't right."

"Nah, I don't need a bodyguard."

"I'm serious."

"So am I. Toby's waiting for you, remember? Coop is likely going nuts at the Easy Breezy right now. Let it go."

After a moment, Vann takes a breath, then turns back to me and nods. "I'll let it go for now. Next time that shit happens around me, I'm saying something."

"Thanks."

Then we climb onto the bike together and off we go.

Usually when we head back to town from the college, we can tear down the causeway like bullets. But tonight—a Saturday night at the end of July—we find ourselves in a slow, noisy line of cars feeding themselves into the already crowded streets of Dreamwood Isle. It takes a full half hour for us to reach the back parking lot of the bar where Vann drops me off. I thank him for the ride there and back, then tell him to say hello to Toby for me. He gives me a smile before taking off, braving the uncharacteristically chaotic traffic tonight, and I'm on my own again.

I have to dodge crowds of people on my way through the doors of the bar, then find myself lost somewhere in the back of the room, overwhelmed by the amount of people. I can't even see Coop until I stand on a chair in the back to get a view over the crowd. He's in the middle of pouring shots when he spots me and gives a smile.

Everything feels better when he's nearby. Not thinking about snide remarks. Can't care less about sugar daddy this or spoiled that. It's just me, Cooper, and our crazy life.

Our crazy, magical, unexpected life in Dreamwood.

I remember something about Mars being sick, which explains why there aren't an extra set of hands helping out. So I jump right in and start bussing tables no one's gotten to yet. Chase waves cheerily at me as he hurries by to take someone's order. I bring a bunch of glasses to the back and start washing them. Duncan is the cook tonight, with a pair of ear buds shoved in, bopping his head to the music, with sweat dripping down his forehead. Chase falls behind with taking orders out, so I get on top of it. I'm not in a uniform. I have no nametag. I just do what needs to be done.

Later on, I push through the back door with two heavy bags of trash and cross the gravel toward the dumpster. Out here, it's practically silent compared to the loud bar. Nearly peaceful. I toss the heavy bags into the dumpster with a grunt, then turn to head back inside.

A moving shadow in the parking lot stops me.

When I look, I see no one there.

I wait, listening. Only distant noise from the beach and the muffled sound of the crowd in the bar can be heard. I decide I'm being paranoid and keep walking—only to then hear the distinct sound of crunching gravel, like two short footsteps, followed by abrupt silence again when I stop. I turn around and look. No one. Not even a stray cat or dog.

It might be my imagination. Maybe it was something settling in the dumpster behind me. But the noises sounded too intentional and go away the second I look for them.

Is someone out there in the parking lot?

Not willing to find out, I race to the door, yank it open, and slip inside. The moment the heavy door slams shut at my back, I feel instant relief.

It's just like that moment outside the movie theater. I thought I heard something. Thought I *saw* something. I'm convinced some instincts will never go away ... no matter how deeply I bury that little demon of my past inside me.

I will always be wary of strange sounds in dark places, as if danger is lurking around every corner.

Creeping noises.

Whispers.

The distinct scuffle of a shoe along the ground, often the telltale noise of someone sneaking up on me while I'm clutching my belongings trying to get a wink of sleep on an old creaky park bench.

I touch my scar again, thinking about that night in San Antonio—that night my heart raced so fast, I thought it was marching its way out of my fucking ears. No matter how many Vanns or Coopers enter my life, I'll never feel safe.

I find myself sitting on the tiled ground in the buzzing dim light of the back utility room, right by the door and the fuse box, knees hugged tightly to my chest. I keep tracing my jagged scar with a finger like I'm reading brail while staring emptily at a long crack in the off-white wall before me. Suddenly, I can't be around all of that noise out there.

I close my eyes and try to imagine safe spaces.

Cooper's house.

Cooper's bed.

Cooper's arms.

I take one deep breath in, then let it out. I do this seven times slowly. The noise of the bar fades away. The hum of a refrigerator nearby goes away, too. After a while, all I can hear is my own breathing and my slowing heartbeat.

The scuffle of a shoe startles me awake. I look up.

Coop peers down at me from the doorway leading back into the kitchen. "You alright?"

"Yeah." After a moment, I get to my feet and quickly brush myself off. "I-I'm fine."

"You sure?"

I realize one of my safe spaces just found me. So I go right up to it and put myself there—right in Cooper's arms, the side of my face pressed to his big, strong, warm chest. He closes his arms tightly around me like a protective cage. I close my eyes. He doesn't ask anything more. He knows what I need. He lets me stay right here in my safe space for as long as I want. The sound of Cooper's strong, measured heart beat soon replaces my own, the only thing I hear, the only thing I feel, and I find myself drifting away.

CHAPTER 19

COOPER

I STROKE HIS HAIR AS WE LIE IN BED TOGETHER.

Listening to him sleep brings me a deep, inner peace. It compares to nothing I've ever known in my life, being able to give him this priceless gift.

I've been playing this dark game in my mind lately. I try to imagine myself without any of my daily luxuries I've taken for granted all these years.

My life without a roof over my head.

Without a bar that supports me.

Without friends I can trust. Without the responsibility of those plants on my back porch.

Without the safety of a bed or the assurance of food to eat every morning, afternoon, and night.

No matter how much Sean demanded that I never feel pity for him, I try to imagine the nightmare he has lived in. I imagine living that fearful, lonesome nightmare for just a single day. Then for a week. Then for a month.

Then for five long months.

I wonder what his life was like before that nightmare. Was it even worse? I've been forced to fill in the blanks of his past between the tiny details he has let slip. His abusive father. His vacant mother who left him alone with that bad man. How terrible his life must have been. Was there ever a flicker of joy in his childhood? Good times? Laughter?

How can a parent throw their child away? What kind of hell must they live in to do that to their own blood?

"Coop?"

I thought he was asleep. "Yeah?"

"You're squeezing me too tight."

I didn't even realize I'd gone from stroking his hair to holding him in my arms. I relax my grip. "Sorry."

"Don't be sorry for it." I hear the smile in his words. "I like it. As long as I can still breathe, you can squeeze me as much as you want."

I smile down at him and resume cuddling—this time a touch gentler.

But my mind still finds no rest.

I want to know why he went from running around the bar doing things tonight to hiding in the back room. I want him to tell me without me prying it out of him. Something happened. I'm convinced of it. Even when I asked how his photoshoot went, he gave me a vague "It went great" then resumed eating the wings we brought home as I stared at him suspiciously over my can of beer.

I want to know what really made him leave home. How bad was it? Do I have to hunt down his dad and make him see the beautiful human being he's missing out on? If I see the man, I'm afraid I wouldn't be able to hold back from doing something I'll regret, something that's totally not in my nature, something violent and red-eyed.

It might be better Sean doesn't tell me.

There's no telling what I might do.

Sunday morning after breakfast, Sean and I take a long walk down the beach. There are so many people here this weekend, many of them have found their way up to the far reaches of Sugarberry Beach, so we aren't as alone as we might want to be. Sean doesn't seem to care; he basks in the morning sunshine in just a tank top and shorts with his new sunglasses on. With him having no Sunday gigs and me leaving the responsibilities of the bar to Chase for the day, Sean and I are free to do what we want. For right now, that's enjoying a nice walk on the semi-crowded beach as if we're the only ones here.

"What are your parents like?" asks Sean as we walk.

I glance at him curiously.

He kicks playfully at the sand, hands in his pockets. "I know what *you're* like. I wonder what *they're* like."

"Hmm. My dad was easygoing. My mom, less so, but she was the one who kept him anchored and balanced."

"Did they run the bar before you did?"

I nod. "It was my dad's pride and joy. My mom did the books. I learned everything from them … but I think I took a lot of it for granted."

"What do you mean?"

"I mean …" After a thought, I shrug. "I was young like you once, y'know. Young and springy and … as horny as an animal. I've told you about it."

"So?"

"So I didn't take my life seriously. I played too much. I just wonder if I … maybe should've listened to my parents more when they were around."

"When they were around …?"

"Oh, sorry. No, they're not dead. Grandma—my dad's mom—got too ill to take care of herself, so my parents had to make the difficult decision to move to Florida to help out, trusting the bar to me. It was a while ago."

"Do you wish they hadn't gone?"

"I miss them, if that's what you mean. But I was happy to take over the bar. My parents were ready to retire." I walk up to the water and stop, letting the waves rush over my feet as I gaze out at the horizon. "Sometimes, I come out here, right up here to the shoreline, and I look out there and … and pretend I can see them way across the Gulf of Mexico. I pretend they're waving back from that distant west coast of Florida."

"They must be proud of you."

I glance at Sean, who has come up to my side. I realize who I'm telling all of this to. He has none of the parental connection I just described. Not even a dream of it to cling to. At once, all my thoughts and feelings from last night flood back into my mind like storm clouds.

I put my arm around Sean and pull him to my side. He loses his balance a bit and has to cling to me for support. "You are one special guy, Sean. Don't forget that."

"Am I?"

"And I'm proud of you." I rub his side. "I feel like the luckiest man in the world, to have gotten to see you bloom the way you have this summer. I want you to chase all your dreams, each and every one of them."

"Do you ever wonder what people think of us?"

I frown at him. "No."

"Well, I do." Another wave rushes in to cover our feet, then gently recedes. "Even right now, I wonder if there are people on this beach, people behind us, who look at us and think I'm, like, a twink with a daddy fetish. Or if they take

221

a look at you and judge you, thinking you're some lonely man who plays with jailbait ..."

"What? No."

"Or what if they think we're *actually* father and son? Is that weird?"

"Where is this coming from, Sean?" I turn to him. "Did someone say something to you?"

He sighs. "Never mind."

"Tell me. I'm not mad. Just tell me."

"I'm just thinking too much, that's all." He looks up at the sky, takes a breath, then sighs again. "I'm just thinking too much and ruining our day off."

"If someone said something to you, or if someone on the island is making you feel a certain way ..."

"They're not on the island."

"So someone *did* say something?" I press on.

"Just forget it. Please. Forget I said anything. It's just the little ugly creature inside me talking." He slips out from under my arm and continues walking. I stare after him for a moment. He stops and peers over his shoulder, suddenly appearing cheery. "Hey, I was thinking we could go to the taqueria for lunch today. Maybe ask how Mars is doing."

I don't know how I'm going to get it out of him.

How can I help Sean if he won't tell me what's up?

For now, I drop it. "Of course." Then I catch up to him, and off we go, continuing our stroll down the beach.

Taqueria Tía Juanitas is a hot spot at the far end of the boardwalk, right on the corner, visible from the causeway leading to the mainland. With tables sprinkled out on the boardwalk in front of the restaurant and a beautiful yellow-and-white-striped awning extending out from the front door lined with exotic plants, it's a place that easily attracts customers with an appetite for the best damned Tex-Mex in the state. We take an outside spot right by the water, with a large umbrella that only covers half our table thanks to the odd angle of the sun, but the view is too beautiful to resist. I get the pleasure of listening to Sean moan and squirm as he enjoys his fajitas, which were brought out sizzling with their mouthwatering, savory aroma.

Alana, Mars's mother who looks like her twin sister, tries to comp our meal, but I insist on paying, considering how much Mars helps me out. Alana and I go way back. We had (and blew off) so many classes back in school. Our hijinks even got us sent to the principal's office a couple of times. Alana doesn't get to chat with us for long, sadly, considering how busy it is, but it's always great to catch up with her. For our businesses being so close together, it's a wonder we don't hang out as often as we used to.

"Our one-month anniversary already passed."

I flinch from my thoughts. "What?"

After a sip from his Coke, Sean smiles at me. "Over a month since I stole your nuts for the last time."

"Oh. Time really flies by, huh?"

"I'm not the anniversary-celebrating type of guy." He stirs his drink with his straw for a moment. "But if I was, how do you think we'd celebrate our one month?"

I fold my arms on the table and shrug, squinting in the sunlight. "Not sure. It's been a long time since I've been with anyone, so—"

"You mean ever since dart-thrower?"

That's what we call Drake. We never actually say his name. Come to think of it, I can't remember whether or not I even told Sean what it is. "Yeah. Since dart-thrower."

"Your romance skills are rusty, then. You're totally out of practice. Poor me." Sean stirs his drink some more. We finished eating a while ago. Our crumb-filled plates rest on the table with an empty basket between us that once housed Alana's special brand of delicious homemade tortilla chips. "I thought the phone was, like, maybe a gift to celebrate it. You gave it to me on the exact date of our one month."

"Really? Well, it wasn't a gift like that. It was more a practical gift. Something I thought you needed." I smirk. "I don't need an occasion to give you something you need."

"Thanks. It helps me feel a bit more human again." He traps some Coke into the straw with a finger, then brings the end of it to his mouth and playfully releases it. With a smile, he gazes at the water appearing thoughtful. "Can't put a price on that."

I tilt my head, trying to get a read on him. "Did you want to do something more special tonight? Is that it?"

"I wasn't trying to suggest anything. Just being funny."

"If you want something from me …"

"You'll get it for me? Is that what you want to say?" He isn't looking at me. "I'm not a starry-eyed schoolboy expecting monthly gifts and an abundance of attention. I'm an adult, like you. A realistic adult who knows how the world works … who knows some things aren't possible." He goes back to stirring his drink, then laughs suddenly. "Can you imagine that? Like, if a phone is my one-month gift, what are you planning to get me for our one-year? A car?" His eyes meet mine. The laughter fades. "Would you buy me a car, Coop?"

He's not acting right. "Do you think I'm trying to buy your affection or something?"

"Would you have been so quick to help me that night if I was ugly?"

"What?"

"It's an honest question. I'm not even sure I mind if the answer is 'no'. Maybe I'd even respect an honest answer. You and I gave this some time, haven't we? Are you happy with me? Do I make you happy? Or … Or am I just—"

I reach across the table and take his hand. "Sean."

"Cooper …" He sighs as he stares at our clasped hands. "I think we should—"

Before he can finish that terrifying sentence, a shadow falls over the table, and a sweet old lady lets out a wiggly, happy little sound at us. "Sonny, boy, is that you??"

Sean looks up from his drink.

His eyes flash. His mouth hangs open. "Ma'am ...?"

"It *is* you!" she sings happily, this old woman with big white cotton balls for hair, pale papery skin, and oversized sunglasses. "How wonderful! I said we would run into each other sometime soon, but I didn't expect to actually—Oh, what a *splendid* Sunday afternoon this has become!"

Sean has trouble speaking. "Y-Yeah. Wow. I didn't ... I didn't expect to, uh ... to see you again so soon, ma'am."

"Didn't I tell you my name? It's Pearl. Oh!" Her face lights up like a merry bonfire upon seeing me. "Is this him? Is this your Uncle Don? Hi there, Don! I'm—"

Before she says her name, her eyes fall on our hands.

Our clasped hands.

Sean retracts his at once, returning to stirring his drink with his straw. Mine are left on the table, where I stare up at the strange old lady and wait for her to continue.

When she does, her voice is changed. "I'm Pearl. I met your, um... your sweet nephew on a bus ride many weeks ago—I can't even say how many." She frets. "*Are* you his uncle? Oh, dear. Did I mistake you for his uncle?"

Sean stares at me across the table in a panic.

He keeps stirring his drink, silent, sweating.

I don't know what comes over me. I have no idea what dark magic I'm handling here by playing along. "Y-Yes, of course, I'm his Uncle John. Hi there, Pearl, ma'am. Thank you very much for your words about my nephew. He … He is very sweet, indeed."

"John?" Her eyebrows lift up high over her sunglasses. "Or wasn't it Don? Did I mishear you?"

"Don." I laugh it off. "Too much time in the sun."

"Ah, yes, of course." She perks back up, though I can't help but notice she's clutching her purse to her chest now. "Yes, very sweet, your nephew. I got the fast impression he has a heart of gold, this one." She turns her full attention back to Sean. "My husband and I—you remember him, the snore monster?—we've been staying here the whole week. I'm surprised I'm only just now running into you! We have a—oh, what's the place called, I keep forgetting—a room at the Ellis … the Elvis … *Elysian*, that's it. The Elysian. It's right across the street from the beach. I'm turning into a crispy strip of bacon every day by the resort pool."

Sean smiles. "That sounds really nice, ma'am."

"Call me Pearl, please. 'Ma'am'. I'm no '*ma'am*', ha! When did you get so formal suddenly?" She lets out a soft, mirthful laugh, then lifts her sunglasses off her face and buries them in her cottony hair. "If you need a tan, you just come find me by the pool. I'm even there in the evenings after dinner. I have *so* many books to read."

"Thanks."

Pearl smiles. Then her eyes shift to me with reluctance. "I'd better get back to shopping for all my granddaughters. Need to check with my son about a ... about a thing or two. His daughters are the fussiest, bless their hearts—*and his*. I never know what to get the girls that won't end up getting tossed to the regift pile." She giggles and shakes her head, then puts a hand on Sean's shoulder. He looks up at her, as if startled by the touch. "Enjoy your afternoon, sonny. You know where to find me."

When the old woman leaves, Sean is left staring at his glass of watered-down Coke with a vacant, cheerless look on his face. He says nothing.

I speak softly. "Who was that?"

It takes him a minute to respond. "No one."

"You met her on a bus?"

"Bus from San Antonio."

I feel like I have to be careful here for some reason. "Cool. She seems like a nice lady."

"She knew who I was the second she met me. That I was in trouble. On the run. On my own. I could see the pity in her eyes. She gave me a sandwich and bottle of water, and she offered me a place to stay." He stares down at the table. "I almost said yes."

The look on his face breaks my heart. "And you ended up here instead."

"I made up some story about an Uncle Don and his two dogs living in a nice house by the beach. Did you see the way she looked at me? At us? At you?" Sean fidgets with his straw. "This was always a pipedream, wasn't it?"

"What do you mean?"

"Being foolish enough to believe this could actually work. A respectable career. Dreamwood Isle. You and me. It's all just a stupid fantasy from a stupid kid."

"No, it's not. Sean, look at me."

"A stupid, stupid kid."

I reach over the table and take his hands once again, wet from the condensation off his glass. He meets my eyes. "Listen to me. You're not stupid. This is not a pipedream. None of this situation is your fault. You don't deserve to carry the burden of your bad parents or what they've done to you. You deserve happiness. You deserve comfort. Sean, you deserve paradise."

"Maybe you were the sweet one all along, to entertain this fantasy," he says. "The moment you met me, you were trying to get rid of me. If there was a vacant room at one of those places, we wouldn't be in this position today. Maybe you should have trusted your gut and gotten rid of me."

"Stop it, Sean. This isn't—"

"Even that first weekend, you were trying to get rid of me again." He looks up from his hands and stares at me. "You remember the night we went to the street fair? You wanted me to meet more guys my age. 'They're all over the island' you kept telling me. You left me with Toby and Vann and ran to the bar with some made-up excuse, some made-up emergency. Remember?"

I thought he believed it. I guess I was more transparent than I realized. "I wasn't trying to get rid of you, Sean."

"I'm not mad at you. I respect what you're trying to do. It's more than anyone's ever done for me before. But ..."

He pulls his hands away.

I feel my heart dropping. "Sean ..."

"We tried this out between us for a while. We gave ourselves time together." He closes his eyes. "I think we need to try some time apart now."

I asked for this. I shouldn't be angry. I shouldn't fight it. I literally wanted him to be on his own and experience his own life and meet guys his age when it was all new. So why is every nerve in my body fighting to cling to him? Why am I hurt? Why am I feeling angry?

Do I feel guilty for keeping him to myself?

Am I just as selfish as every other man who came into his life?

Shouldn't I support his decisions?

"Can I say something first?"

Sean looks at me, waiting.

I take a breath. "You are, and have always been, free to do what you want. I won't stop you. But I won't close my

door, either. I'm keeping my promise to you, even still …
even if you choose to get up from this table and go. I'm not
pushing you away. I'm not getting rid of you. Think it over
for a bit, Sean. Don't be rash. You have all the time in the
world to figure out what you want. It's no one's decision
but yours."

Sean looks away for a moment. His foot bounces in
place under the table.

Then he says, "I need to go for a walk."

CHAPTER 20

SEANY

I NEED TO GO FOR A WALK?

Really?

I've made it all the way to the north end of the island, standing on the edge of a different kind of boardwalk that lines a rocky coast with the Hopewell Fair protruding into the water, along with a number of large houses and condos whose monthly mortgages I can't even begin to fathom. I sit on the curb across from all of that, hugging my knees and staring at the sky. Distant chimes and cheers of games, rides, and people having fun float in the air.

I've had my little walk.

And I still don't feel good about anything at all.

Not about the old lady finding me and looking like she secretly wanted to save me from Satan Cooper, who most certainly is *not* my uncle. Not about how Lily and SJ made me feel. Not about the phone in my pocket, nor this joke of a modeling career I think I'm starting now, nor my dream of someday feeling like a normal human being again.

The only thing I feel good about is Coop.

And I'm throwing that away, too.

He thinks I'll be happier on my own with guys my age. I think he'll be happier not having to deal with the constant judgment and handling of a messed up runaway like me. We were doomed since the night he foolishly decided to take me in. He didn't ask for this. He didn't even want this, not at first.

I wish I was more like the others I've met on the street. My life would be so much easier if I could just go with the flow, take everything that's given to me no matter what it costs others, and bear zero guilt. I'd kick back in Cooper's house and eat and drink my fill all damn summer. I'd take everything he gives me without the intention of paying back a cent. I would have laughed along with SJ and Lily, because if I was someone like that, I would have long since killed my emotions and felt nothing.

But I'm not that kind of guy.

I'm cursed with an annoying conscience or something.

An hour later, I notice Cooper hasn't called me. Two hours later, still no call. It seems like the man is respecting my space. I think having a conscience is Coop's curse, too. He's too good of a man.

It's early evening when I find myself at a familiar spot I don't think I've been around since before I met Coop. It's a gas station with an attached sandwich place, and right by the curb is a long bench with some lawyer's advertisement slapped on the front. I crouch on the bench, my ass in the lawyer's face, with my knees hugged to my chest as I lazily watch the occasional car go by.

One car stops at the red light in front of me, and in its backseat is some guy my age. He's laughing at something that was just said in the car, happy tears in his eyes, when he looks over and catches my gaze. For some odd reason, I don't look away. I just stare back at him, deadpan, ghoulish and blank. His face slowly relaxes as he watches me, for a moment looking hypnotized. I can't say what he's thinking, but I hear someone in the front ask everyone in the car if they want to hit up the club tonight. Everyone else in the car answers except him—his entire focus locked on me like I just became the most interesting thing in the world.

I wonder if he's thinking how I ended up crouched on a park bench instead of riding in the backseat of a car with my own friends, carefree, happy, racing off to a nightclub.

I wonder if he has any idea what he's got.

234

If he has any idea how lucky he is.

The red light goes green, and the car tears off. I watch it go, still hugging my knees to my chest. I watch it until it goes around the corner and vanishes from sight.

I think that's when I make the decision.

It's time for me to leave Dreamwood Isle.

"God dang it, fuck me, are you serious??"

I turn around. A cute guy in skinny jeans and a bright yellow t-shirt stands there holding a sandwich in one hand and the lid to a cup in the other. The cup itself is at his feet, having slipped from his grip, spilled across the pavement. His peachy skin is flushed with anger at the cheeks, and his short brown hair looks like it was styled nicely a few hours ago, but now lays as tousled and troubled as his expression.

He's not having a great day.

When he looks up, he realizes I witnessed his tantrum. "Sorry," he nearly growls, then kicks at the pavement. "I was looking forward to drinking that, too. Fuckin' figures."

"They might give you a replacement," I point out. "The lady inside is nice."

"Wasn't a lady who served it."

"Oh. If it's the strict guy with a goatee, you're shit out of luck."

He sighs. "Shit out of luck, then." He frowns when he realizes some of his drink splattered all over his shoes. "Fuck me."

"Shout that out enough times around here, someone's bound to obey."

"Ha," he delivers dryly, then goes to a nearby trashcan to throw away the lid. "Guess I'll get another." Just as he's about to go, he stops, reconsiders, then glances back at me. "You waiting on someone, or—?"

I shrug.

He frowns. "That's not an answer. Anyway, I'm going to get myself another drink. You want anything? I planned on eating this in my car, but I hate eating alone, so—"

"I'm not getting in your car with you, you creep."

His frown deepens. "I'm not inviting you into my—For fuck's sake, is everyone on this island an asshole? Never mind, forget it." He heads back to the sandwich place.

I smirk, then face the street again, resting my chin on my knees. The sun is still in the sky, but it's reaching that time of the evening when the streetlamps get ready to flick on. It's not an ideal time to leave town. It'll be night soon.

But I'm not sure I can go back to Cooper's place. Not with the way I'm feeling right now. I should probably give him this phone back, though. He could maybe return it.

I can try my luck with the old lady. She told me exactly where she's staying for a reason; she's expecting to be my lifeline in a pinch.

But she's still a wildcard. It could just be a trap.

Everything feels like a trap.

A small plastic bag drops onto the bench next to me. I turn to it, perplexed. It's a wrapped sandwich from the gas station place behind me with a drink sitting next to it.

When I turn, I find the guy staring down at me. "Sorry. I decided it was *me* being the asshole." He comes around the bench and sits at the other end of it, leaving enough space between us for a family of four. "Eat it if you want. Save it for later. Throw it away. Doesn't matter. It's my apology to you, and in this town, you can eat apologies." He opens up his own sandwich and takes a big bite.

It's literally the first rule in any book. You don't drink anything that wasn't made in front of your own eyes. You don't trust any food from strangers, either; certain death or captivity can be a crushed-up pill away, sprinkled between the ham and cheese of any unsuspecting sandwich.

"You know what really gets me?" he goes on through his mouthful. "Fucking first impressions. They're all such bullshit. People get this idea of who you are in, like, the first five seconds of meeting you, and if it happens to be a particularly *shitty* five seconds, then there you go, you're an asshole for life. And it becomes your mission, to prove to the world you aren't that person."

I lift an eyebrow. "It's not that big a deal."

He looks at me. "Huh?"

"My first impression of you. Who cares? You spilled a drink. I'd be pissy about it, too."

He seems confused for a second. "Oh. That? No. That isn't—" He laughs suddenly. "No, that isn't what I meant. I'm not talking about us or that. Who cares. We just met. I'm talking about the love of my life."

"Oh."

"Actually … I shouldn't call him that anymore. He is *not* the love of my life. He's someone I said goodbye to a long, long time ago." The guy takes a huge bite from his sandwich, then chews with anger. "I'm still mad," he says between chomping. "Wish he didn't know me at my worst. I was such a *brat*. Selfish and impulsive. Now, no matter where I go, no matter who I'm fucking, I just keep getting glimpses of that *brat* I used to be. Why can't I let him go? I can't love myself—I can't *accept* myself—unless I say goodbye to that brat, too, that asshole I used to be." He goes for a vigorous sip from his drink, then glances at me. "Sorry, I'm ranting at you and you don't even know me."

"It's fine," I decide with a shrug. "I think I get it."

He takes another bite, then looks at me. "You do?"

"Sure. People have an impression of me because I'm in a relationship with an older guy. At least I *think* I am. They want to call him my sugar daddy. Or they think I'm just whoring myself out for gifts and money."

"Really? That's not a big deal. I was with an older guy, too, back in my day. He was in his late twenties. And I was the hot young ass in town who just graduated high school and had cash to burn one weekend." He shakes his head. "Little did I know that one weekend would change my whole fucking life."

I let go of my knees and sit normally on the bench with a tired sigh. "I've been fighting people's opinions of me for pretty much forever."

He nods. "Same. If it means anything, you sound like a pretty decent guy to me."

"I'm far from decent."

"Don't be so hard on yourself. You're only saying bad stuff about yourself because someone else put those words in your head. Who did that? Asshole parents? I've got two of those. A clique of bad influences for friends? Got those, too. Nothing surprises me anymore. You'll come to learn as you get older that you're a much better person than you think you are. Just ignore those bad voices in your head."

"It isn't so easy to just ignore it."

"I know."

"I just want to be myself and live my stupid little life without prying eyes and questions. But my past haunts me everywhere I go. It clings to me."

"The past is a bitch," he agrees between bites, glaring at the street and shaking his head.

"It is. It really is."

"So how do we let it go, my friend?"

I give him a look. "Friend?"

"There has got to be a way to get past our … past." He pulls something out of his mouth with a disgusted grimace, then flicks it onto the paper with a sigh. "I *said* no pickles."

I shrug. "I don't have an answer. It's why I'm out here by myself, sitting on this stupid bench, debating what my next move is when I skip town."

He looks at me. "Skip town?"

I nod. "Yeah. I think my time here is over. Paradise has had me and let me go."

"No, don't give up yet. You're one of the nice ones. I can tell and I've barely known you five minutes. *Ugh*, you have clearly been hurt by an asshole. Probably by someone like how I used to be. Dreamwood collects driftwood, too. Just be smart enough to tell the difference and don't get discouraged so fast, man. You gotta toughen up."

"I'm tough enough. It's not about being tough." I look away. "It's just time I start being realistic and … and face whatever the real world out there has in store for me."

"'The real world out there' …? Honey, the real world's right here, too. Dreamwood is just as real. What exactly are you picturing on the other side of that causeway? A boring job? A boring boyfriend your age? Being just like everyone else? Fucking overrated. Wake up. You're badass the way you are. Look at you, smart enough to not eat something a stranger gave you. Shit … you're making my younger self look like a real dumbass. I was such a clueless twat."

I find myself thinking about that old lady, about Pearl. I ate the sandwich she gave me. Every last bite. Chugged most of the water and put the rest away in that backpack I used to have until it was stolen one night while I slept.

"Wanna hear something truly pathetic?" he asks with a snort. "I've dragged myself to this island every weekend for a whole damned month with the same intention … then keep chickening out."

I look at him. "What intention is that?"

"Doesn't matter. Too chicken to do it." He shakes his head. "Maybe my own advice is shit. The island is trying to tell me something and I won't listen. I should leave, too. Like you. But for good this time."

I lean forward, elbows on my knees, and prop my head up by the chin. Am I really leaving Dreamwood? Is it all over? The island feels sleepy and abandoned in this area, making me feel as if it's already forgotten me. No more cars have gone by since that last one. I wonder if that kid made it to the club with his laughing friends yet. I wonder if he dances badly.

I wonder if this is my last sunset in Dreamwood.

From the other side of the street, I spot an approaching guy—someone in an old tank top and shorts, messy hair, with a patchwork of stubble across his cheeks and neck.

Upon recognizing him, I lose all train of thought.

Whatever sliver of comfort still lived in me is gone.

He stops in the middle of the street with his hands in his pockets. "Hey there, buddy. Long time no see."

The most unsettling thing about Ice is his lack of facial expression. He doesn't look sly, nor evil, nor kind. He's a blank slate at all times. You never really know what he's planning until you're already in the middle of it.

My acquaintance on the bench looks up at Ice, frowns, then glances at me with mild curiosity.

I face Ice. "I'm not your buddy."

"Of course you are. We've been through so much, you and I, so much together." He takes a few more steps across the street, then stops again. "Where's your big lover?"

There's no telling which friend he's referring to. "Are you really so bored that you can't leave me alone?"

"But you're in my part of town. What're you doing in my part of town, huh?"

"You don't own any part of town," I spit back at him. "I can go wherever I want."

"Oh, yeah? You're the big man of the island now, huh? Got yourself a big daddy to take care of you, and now you think you're too good for me, huh? Why're you being so cruel to your friend?" He becomes a drama queen for five seconds, grabbing his heart like I just struck an arrow in it. "Shit, and after all that meaningful time we spent together. I thought you learned how to share."

"Share?"

"Yeah, share. You scored something nice. You've got a man with a house and a bank account. Why can't you just invite your buddy over sometime? C'mon." He's up next to the bench now. "Let me have some of that sugar, too."

"He's not a bag of *sugar*."

"Of course he is. Everyone here is. Have you learned nothing? Buddy, if we're gonna make it here on this island, you gotta learn how to get coconuts out of trees, and I—"

"Doesn't matter," I cut him off. "I'm not gonna be here for much longer anyway."

"What?"

"You heard me." I point at the road. "I'm heading out of town. I'm leaving Dreamwood Isle. You can have all the *sugar* you want."

He seems confused for a moment. Then he laughs as if I just told the funniest joke. "You can't leave yet. Why go before making one last hit?" He plops down on the bench next to me. "I can help you, buddy. Let's do it together."

I get to my feet, putting distance between us. "I don't want your help, Ice."

He stands right up again and gets in my face. "Hey, you're not thinking this through. I protected you when you slept, remember? All those nights, I watched your back. Remember that crazy fucker the day we met? I handled him, too." His face is getting twitchy. This is not a good sign. "Why can't you give back a little? You got something worked out with this sad bartender guy, clearly you made it work, so why are you keeping him all to yourself?"

"Cooper's not a 'scheme' or a job. Cooper's someone I actually care about. A good man with a good heart. He—"

"Bullshit." Flecks of spit hit me in the face as he barks the word. "Good man? Good heart? He's probably a letch who's getting off on having a cute kid like you around."

"He is *not* a letch."

"If you cared about him, then why are you bailing? It's obvious you think it isn't going anywhere. Let me show you how wrong you are. Then we can hit the road together. Hey, if you don't have the guts to do it," he says, changing his tone erratically in an instant, "I can do it myself. Just give me an in, bud. Tell him you're bringing a friend over to hang out tonight. When the man's asleep—*BAM!*" He smacks his hands together. "We clear the bitch out. Cash, jewelry, valuables, whatever he's got around. Then we bail. We'll head up the causeway, grab a ride or hitchhike—with your cute face, that won't be a problem—and I can show you my old spot. I got hookups in Houston, man. I know a pawn shop guy. We're tight as fuck. He'll buy anything. You and I can live big for a while."

There will be no negotiating with Ice. No explaining. No getting through his narrow view of the world. I used to feel bad for him when I knew no one around here. Just like anyone else, he has a story too—a story that led him down a long path to right here. But he refuses to live honorably. He despises good intentions. He treats people like stepping stones and tools. Ice is quick to remind me of all the times he protected me, but fails to remember the times he snapped at me, used me, and took advantage of my naïveté.

I wonder if he's the one who stole my backpack.

He probably sold it for drug money for all I know.

"C'mon, why are you still thinking about it?" The man is growing more irritable by the second. "Let's go down to his house right now and you introduce me. I got the whole script worked out, don't gotta worry about a thing. Thought up a backstory and everything. Let me handle it. We'll cash out on this guy once and for all. You just sit back and—"

I turn around, fetch the sandwich bag and drink off the bench, then offer them to him silently.

Ice stares down. "Huh? The fuck is this?"

"Dinner," I answer simply. "Yours. My gift to you."

He wrinkles up his face. "I don't want a sandwich. I want you to take me to Cooper's house."

"We're not going. You want me to share? I'm sharing what I'm willing to: my dinner." I extend the bag again.

He smacks the bag and drink straight out of my hand, sending them flying into the street. "I *said* I don't *want* a *motherfucking sandwich.*"

Fear lances my heart. I take a tiny step back, only to be reminded the bench is behind me when my heel hits it.

He grabs hold of my shirt, startling me. "Don't be a scared little bitch. Just do what I say, take me to him, and you and I can get the hell off this island."

"Ice …"

From the bench comes another voice: "There goes the *second* drink I bought, splat, to the pavement."

Ice looks at the guy, as if just now noticing he's been sitting there. "Who the fuck are you?"

"Just an asshole on a bench." He crosses his legs, then makes a funny face at Ice. "But I might also be the asshole who's about to ruin your day. Can you do me a favor and look up at the stoplights?"

Ice frowns, annoyed, then glances up.

"Right there, right on the corner, up high. See it? That, my angry little friend, is what they call a *security camera*. You are on that camera. Someone is watching the feed on that camera. Someone is watching you grabbing the shirt of a guy whose food you just knocked out of his hands."

Ice doesn't let go. He only scoffs at the camera, lifts a middle finger to it, then sneers at the guy. "You think they actually pay attention to that shit?"

"Maybe not always. But they certainly are right now." He lifts his phone and gives it a wiggle. "See, my dad is the police chief here, and I just sent him a text as a concerned citizen of Dreamwood Isle. Now he's got your face. Your plan. Your act of aggression against my friend. And if there is *anything* my dad hates, it's a stain on the reputation of a lovely paradise like this." His face goes flat. "My dad deals with stains quicker than that Laundromat across the street."

Ice doesn't look across the street at any laundry place. He just stares challengingly at the guy, as if the two are playing a game of chicken, revving their engines, ready.

Then Ice's fingers slowly uncurl.

My shirt is released.

His eyes meet mine. "You're a pussy, you know that? You're a fucking pussy. Turned as soft as everyone else on this stupid island. I don't need you," he suddenly decides. "I don't need this place." Then he starts marching away.

Even after him grabbing me like that. After all his ugly words. After his threats. I still find myself seeing a human being trapped in a living hell, whose terrible habits were bred out of necessity, out of desperate survival instinct, out of fear. Maybe my emotions do make me weak sometimes.

But I don't want to become him.

I don't want to kill everything inside me that's good.

"Ice," I call out.

He stops halfway down the street and turns.

"You can be better than this, y'know," I shout at him. "You can make something honest out of yourself instead of doing what you're doing, always leaving something behind after taking it for what it's worth. Paradise isn't just for the rich and the *soft*. It can be yours, too. It's not too late."

He stares at me for a while.

I wonder for a moment if he heard what I said.

Then he shouts: "Fuck your paradise." He turns and continues on. I watch as he disappears down the road and around the corner.

I have a strange feeling that this might be the last time I ever see him.

"My dad's not really the police chief."

I turn around, nearly forgetting I'm not alone. "Huh?"

"It was all bullshit. Total bluff. Just scaring him away. That old camera probably hasn't worked since 2002."

"Oh. Wow. Well ... thanks."

The guy crosses his arms. "Cooper, huh? Your man? The fellow you care so much about? The one who's been taking care of you? He's Cooper? *Bartender* Cooper?"

I lift an eyebrow. "You know him?"

The guy gazes off for a moment, takes a deep breath, then lets out a sudden laugh. "Oh, this world ... this funny, hilarious little world we live in." He shakes his head. "No, it's not time for me to leave Dreamwood, not until I do this one final thing. And it's certainly not time for you to leave, either, honey." He turns his bright eyes onto me. "You just gave me my purpose back. I'm here to do something, and thanks to you, I am *not* chickening out this time."

FINALE

COOPER

I DRIVE DOWN CASSANOVA STREET, LOOKING.

I go down Boardwalk four times and Main Street five. I go down Evans Street, Finnegan Street, and Artist Row. I drive past every park. I even get out of the car and look around Cottonwood Cove, certain I might find him in that secluded little nook no one goes. I scan Holiday Street and sit at the entrance to the Hopewell Harbor, wondering if I might catch a glimpse of him somewhere. I roll down Gould Street, thinking I might find him walking to my house. Yorke Street. Salazar Street. Montehugh. I even go halfway down the causeway to the mainland.

My calls go straight to voicemail.

My texts go unanswered.

It's been three hours. I know he wants his space. He's in a strange mental state. The old woman seemed to trigger something inside him. He's spooked. He's afraid and he's doubting himself and his place here.

And now I've lost him.

"No, he doesn't have any gigs tonight that I know of," says Vann over the phone. "Why? Is he okay? Do you need me and Toby to go looking for him?"

"I already looked around for several hours. I'm ..." I rub my eyes, sitting in my car in the parking lot of the Easy Breezy. The sun's setting. "I'm probably overreacting. He went out for a walk a while ago and hasn't come back."

"Are you worried something happened? Dreamwood's a pretty safe place, isn't it? I know I haven't been here that long, but I heard the police are basically twiddling their thumbs all day long seven days a week, except for maybe the occasional drunken disturbance."

I force myself to chuckle at that. I feel so sick. "It's a safe place. Few sketchy characters now and then. A regular druggie I've kicked out of the bar a few times in the past. I just ..." *I just have this terrible feeling Sean has hitched a ride out of Dreamwood, leaving me and this life and all his new friends behind.* But that's a bit of an overshare, so I say: "I'll just wait for him at the bar. Thanks, Vann."

250

I hang up before he says goodbye and stare numbly at the back of the bar, confounded. I drum my fingers on the steering wheel in frustration. I pull my phone back out and try calling Sean again. Straight to voicemail. *His phone died*, I decided. *He didn't charge it last night. It's dead. He can't call me even if he needs to.*

But what if he doesn't need to?

What if he doesn't *want* to?

What if he's gone …?

I get out of my car and head for the back door. As soon as I reach it, out comes Mars with a bag of trash. She sees the look on my face and deflates. "No luck finding him?"

I frown at her. "What're you doing here? Alana said you're sick with a fever."

"Have you never played hooky with your own parents to dodge doing work for them?"

"So … you dodged working at the taqueria in order to do work here …? That makes no sense."

"It's more fun. Even if tonight is deader than corduroy, crop tops, and Julius Caesar." She passes by me, tosses the trash into the dumpster, then returns to the door. "If my dear mama asks, I was never here."

Like mother, like daughter. "You got it."

She tugs open the door, then stops and looks at me. "I know I was kinda hard on him. Like, at first. I didn't trust him. Didn't like him. Scoffed at the mere idea of you doing anything nice for him." Her lips twist into a pout. "I wish I had been nicer at the start."

"You guys are friends now," I remind her. "I'm sure he forgave you for all of that."

She shrugs. "Well, if he really did leave, then I guess it doesn't matter. Damage we've done in the past still leave bad tastes no matter how good things seem now. For all I know, he looks at me every day and wonders if I really like him, or if it's all an act." She shakes her head. "Ugh, I should've been, like, way less of a judgy mean girl when he was around. He deserved more."

"You're talking about him like he's dead."

She eyes me. "Sorry." She takes a step inside, then peers back at me again. "Y'know ... you're the guy on the island everyone comes to for advice. Every lost soul. Every love-starved boy. You're always the one with the answers. But who's there to tell *you* what to do when you're lost?"

I struggle to reply, then finally retort with: "Who says I'm lost?"

She shakes her head. "Never mind. Hey, if he shows up and everything turns out alright, forget I said any of this." Then she heads in.

I stay by the door for a while, Mars's words lingering.

I guess I *am* lost.

The moment I step inside and let the heavy door shut at my back, Chase appears. "Boss! Boss, boss, boss. I had an issue while you were gone, a nasty issue, and I resolved it, but I'm not sure if I resolved it right, and I—Oh, you look like you're constipated or something."

I put my hands on Chase's shoulders. "Whatever it was that happened while I was gone, I'm confident you handled it perfectly."

"Uh, 'perfectly' isn't the word I'd use, but—"

"You need to have more confidence in yourself, Chase. I rely on you a lot around here."

"You do?"

"Yeah." I give him a pat. "You're a good man with a good head on your shoulders. A bit distracted at times, but smart when it counts."

"Smart when it counts? Sounds good ... I think."

I move past him and into the kitchen. August, our usual cook, is working tonight, except right now "working" isn't the operative word; he's sitting on a turned-over bucket scrolling through his phone with one earbud in and the other hanging down his chest. "'Sup, boss," he says upon seeing me. "Slow as hell tonight."

I push through the swinging door into the bar, where I confirm there isn't a damned soul in sight. It's only fitting after combing the quiet town for the past hour looking for Sean that I don't find anyone here either. Not even Jonah and Kent who like throwing darts Sunday evenings.

The door flies open.

For half a second, my heart leaps into my throat.

Until I realize it's just Adrian. "Dude, what the balls is up with tonight?"

"You farted and scared everyone on Sugarberry away."

"Manager wanted us to close up, but I thought I'd see how you're doing over here. Obviously not much better." He saunters inside wearing his Thalassa uniform complete with apron and glances around. "Where's my brother? Isn't he usually here with Jonah?"

"Was just thinking that. Not tonight, I guess."

"Feels like everyone's ditched the island."

The words make my blood run cold. I check my phone just in case I missed a buzz or notification. Nothing. "The summer's coming to an end," I mutter, staring at the blank screen resentfully. "Fall will be on us soon."

"Slower times," agrees Mars, appearing at the counter next to me and letting out a yawn.

"I don't mind slow times," says Adrian as he comes up to the bar and folds his big arms on the counter. "Gives me more time to spend with my man."

Mars perks up. "You guys set a date yet?"

"Whoa, whoa. One thing at a time. No need to—"

"Hey, is this where the party's happening?" asks Chase as he emerges from the back. "By the way, I think August fell asleep on a bucket of pickles. Should we prank him or leave him be? Oh, hi, Adrian! Are we talking about your wedding? What's going on?"

Adrian gives him a hard look. "Why in the hell are *you* still single? If a pretty-faced, muscle-dork shorty like Finn can keep a man, there's no reason in the world you can't."

Chase blinks his pretty eyes. "Huh?"

Mars sighs on his behalf. "Adrian, it isn't even close to being the same. Finn and Theo are high school sweethearts. They're only together by default. Besides, they fight all the time, and I doubt they're even in love."

"Damn, girl," cries Adrian. "That's some harsh shit."

"It's some *real* shit," says Mars right back. "No sugar coating. Whenever I see Finn, I don't see a happy guy in a happy relationship. I see chaos and sadness in his eyes. It's a bit like a hectic weekend night when Chase is left to work the kitchen 'cause August and Duncan both called in sick."

Chase gasps. "Hey! That only happened *once* …!"

"Besides, even if Finn *wasn't* with Theo, his family is well-off, he's basically the unofficial prince of Dreamwood if you think about it, and his dad owns Hopewell Harbor and Fair. He can have any guy he wants."

"You're just jaded about lovers because you don't have anyone either," says Chase.

"No, I'm not."

"Hell yeah, you are. You're lonely and taking it out on all us innocent people around you."

"You don't think I get hit on? Gay women exist, too,

y'know, and—"

The two keep bickering back and forth as I, yet again, find myself pondering on Mars's words. Half to myself, I quietly ask, "So … what exactly does a happy guy in a happy relationship look like?"

Perhaps it was the somber tone of my voice, but both Mars and Chase go quiet, their argument ended at once. It seems like no one is sure what to say to that.

Then Mars lets out a sigh. "I wasn't talking about you and Sean. Y'all are adorable."

"Really adorable," agrees Chase.

Adrian sucks in his bottom lip in thought, then leans over the counter. "This is where you're probably expecting me to make a dumb 'daddy-son' joke about you guys, but if I'm being honest here, fuck, even *my* heart's warmed by the sight of you two. Where the hell is he, anyway? Has he been a bad boy? Did you send him home on timeout?" He chortles at himself. "Okay, *there's* the joke."

Mars, knowing the situation, lets out a sigh. "Shut up, Adrian, you're such an idiot."

He squints questioningly at her, then looks at me with alarm. "Wait … *Is* there trouble in paradise? Did y'all get into a fight or something?"

Before I can answer, the doors to the bar swing wide open. Everyone turns.

Sean steps inside, hands in his pockets.

My heart soars into the sky the moment I see him.

Then Drake walks in right behind.

And my heart crashes down through the floor.

Adrian and Mars stare at them, saying nothing. Sean and Drake stare back, the pair of them remaining at the door while my insides writhe around like restless snakes, trying (and failing) to produce a reason in the world why those two would arrive at my bar—together.

From the register, the ever so clueless Chase waves at them. "Don't be shy, you guys! Come on in! We're open!" The silence persists, during which Chase seems to slowly assess that something isn't right.

I come around the counter and stop. Sean keeps his sullen, guarded eyes on me. "Hey, Coop," he finally says after a while.

Hey, Coop?

After spending the last three hours thinking the worst?

Trying not to fathom that Sean vanished from my life?

Hey, Coop??

"Hey, Sean," I return, suppressing my internal screams. I don't acknowledge Drake. I don't ask what they're doing together. There's only one damned thing that matters right now. "Are you alright?"

Sean averts his gaze.

That doesn't make me feel good.

I finally turn my eyes to Drake. "Why are you here?"

Drake lifts a hand up for a pitiful little wave. "Hi."

"The last time you walked out those doors, you said it would be the very last time."

"I did," he agrees. "And then ... I realized I had some unfinished business."

"And that's me? I'm your unfinished business?"

"Well, frankly, yes." Drake turns to Sean. "And thanks to this guy right here who was a second away from fleeing the island on foot, I finally have the courage to do it." His voice turns soft as he faces me. "To do what's right."

Mars, Chase, and Adrian have been huddled at the bar watching all of this play out like a scandalous game show before their unblinking eyes.

Sean looks at Drake, then me, something clicking into place. "You guys know each other ...?"

I make a face. "Dart-thrower."

Sean sits with that for a second, then goes wide-eyed as he turns to Drake. "Wait, you're his ex?"

"Yep. I'm his Ghost of Summer Past." Drake strolls partway toward me, his eyes appearing wistful. "Y'know, after that night when I told you to meet me at Sunnyview to talk, and you didn't show up, I decided it was going to be my fate to just live with the guilt and regret forever. Just like you wanted." He shakes his head. "But something kept bugging me. *You* kept bugging me. If I'm being completely honest here, I was probably entertaining some insane idea that you and I might reunite, miraculously make up, and try our hand at a serious relationship again. I truly thought that could happen if I showed you how much I'd matured over the years." He sucks on his tongue. "So … yes, I broke my promise. I came back here every weekend ever since. But I couldn't bring myself to face you for some reason. It became this … very sad routine of sitting in an overpriced hotel room with a book wondering what the hell I'm doing, finding I'm yet again unable to muster up the courage to face you … then grabbing a sandwich on my way out of this town on another sad Sunday evening. It wasn't until today—until I ran into *this* young fellow upon grabbing my last sad Sunday sandwich ever—that I realized a sobering fact: I don't want you back. I think I never wanted you back." He meets my eyes. "I just wanted you to be happy."

Sean glances down at the floor, looking as if he's still trying to put all the pieces together. My entourage of staff and friends remain as silent audience members at the edges of their seats. And I …

I'm not sure what I'm feeling right now.

"Let's face it," Drake goes on. "We're all stuck. I can't move on until I make it right somehow between us. You haven't moved on because you're still wounded from what I did and never got the answers you deserved. And this guy right here?" He throws a thumb over his shoulder at Sean, who looks up. "He just talked back to a crazy-eyed druggie who wanted to rob you in your sleep, Coop. Sean stood up for you. He defended your honor like a fucking *knight*." Drake laughs and shakes his head as he gives Sean a once-over. "But he's stuck, too. And he needs your help, Coop. Please let me do this for you guys. Let me do this one good thing. I know it doesn't make up for all of the bad, but it's obvious from the way you look at each other that it isn't Sean's time to leave this island, and it isn't your time to let him go. Please. Fight for each other."

I gaze at Sean, lost in his heavy, emotional eyes. "You were really about to leave Dreamwood?"

Sean's voice is so small when he answers. "I ... I don't know what I was going to do."

"You said you were just going for a walk."

"I was. Then I just ... *kept* walking." He peers down at his shoes.

"Is it because of me? Something I did or said?"

"No."

"Was it that Pearl lady?"

"Not completely."

"And who's this druggie? Has he been giving you a hard time? I said I can protect you, Sean. Whoever it is."

"You don't have to worry about him. He's gone." Sean glances at Drake. "Your ex pretended his dad was the chief of police and scared him straight off the island."

I give Drake a questioning look.

Drake shrugs. "Either the guy was gullible, or I'm just a skilled liar."

"You're a skilled liar," I say, solving the mystery for him. After he frowns, I turn back to Sean. "Please tell me what's going on then, if it's not any of those things."

"I know you want to help me," murmurs Sean, bowing his head. "You care about me. You'd fight for me. But ..." He sighs. "You can't fix what's wrong with me. Sorry," he says to Drake suddenly. "I don't know what you expected, bringing me here, but it doesn't change anything. It doesn't fix who I am. I ... I don't ..." He faces me again. I watch him fight back tears. "I don't belong here, Coop."

"You fucking kidding me?" cries out Mars.

Everyone turns.

She hops onto the counter and swings her legs over. "I, for one, would like to argue the point that this place is the *only* place you belong. I like the guys here, don't get me wrong. Skipper and his friends can be fun when they're not stoned. Toby and Vann, they're sweet or whatever. Chase is a ditz. But I was bored outta my *mind* in this little town until you walked through those doors, my Seany-boy." She spreads her hands. "You belong here. With us."

"I second that," says Chase, "except for the ditz part."

"Yeah, you're pretty damned alright," says Adrian.

"We're all your family," Mars goes on. "That should go without saying, damn it. And we got your back, Sean.

Your whole back. Every inch of it, too. Even the parts you don't like."

Sean glances at each of them. His eyes remain stony and unsure.

I'm not sure whether this is the way to convince him.

It's like a group attack. All of us, aggressively insisting on what's best for him. Telling him what the right choice is. Shoving our love in his face—even if that love is real.

He's the one who truly needs to decide.

I come up to him without saying anything. He turns to me with his lost eyes, doggy-paddling to mine through a pool of uncertainty and doubt.

I extend my hand. "Can I show you something?"

He drops his gaze to it. I think he's still fighting back tears. After a long moment, he finally takes my hand. With his hand in mine, I lead him to the door, then leave behind the Easy Breezy and everyone there.

Alone, across a beach without a soul on it, I walk with him to the nearby Quicksilver Strand. We walk in silence, only the breeze from the Gulf in our ears. Our footsteps are soft in the part-dirt, part-sand path we walk. Once we reach the smooth planks of the boardwalk, our footsteps seem to mimic our hearts with their gentle, patient cadence. Most of the Quicksilver shops and restaurants are closed, just a few workers still in the midst of their closing duties.

One end of the boardwalk has a short pier that juts out

into the water, lined with a pair of decorative benches. It's there that we take a seat and enjoy the quiet together.

Sean's the first to break the silence. "Why did you bring me out here?"

"Thought you might want a break."

"A break from what?"

"All of that *pressure* back at the bar. Drake giving half a sermon. Mars going on and on. Whether you choose to stay here with us ... or try your luck on the next town ... I want it to be your decision. Not theirs."

Sean considers that. "And ... you took me all the way out here just for that?"

"I also wanted to get in one last stroll with you down the boardwalk, hand-in-hand." I turn my face to him. "Just in case."

He looks at me, too.

The bench is small. We're pressed close together, our sides touching, still holding hands. Two tall lampposts over us and the pale moonlight scattered over the water provide the only light. It's more than enough to see the deep look in Sean's eyes upon hearing those words.

I lift my hand to his forehead and brush away bangs. He closes his eyes. "There's no hurry at all," I remind him. "Here in Dreamwood, everything goes at its own pace. The pace can be as slow as the tide. Or quick as lightning. You decide what direction you take in life, Sean. From now on, you decide everything."

Sean looks away, thinking that over. The rush of the waves fills our ears for a while.

Then he says, "Drake isn't that bad."

I lift an eyebrow. "What?"

"He isn't the monster I was expecting, judging from all the things you told me about him."

Even I have to admit, if it wasn't for the absurdly lucky timing of circumstance, Sean might be on the other side of the causeway by now, lost to the mainland and the horrors of the unknown.

"But I'm only meeting the new him," Sean adds. "The more mature version of him. I didn't see what he was like back then. I didn't see the monster that broke your heart. The thought of that ... it gives me ..." His face contorts, making him appear conflicted. "... it gives me hope."

"Hope?"

"Could that be me?" He glances my way, his eyes full of moonlight, just as a wave crashes beneath us. "If I live here, will the person I was no longer exist? Will he be gone for good?"

I take hold of his hand with both of mine, rubbing it. "I have to be honest with you, Sean ... I don't know if that's possible. We can't change who we are or where we came from. But ... maybe we shouldn't want to, either. What's the point of regret? The pain you lived brought you here.

The pain I lived left my heart open to you." I look at him. "Without it, we may never have met."

He watches as I rub his hand, his eyes as stormy and conflicted as the waves beneath us.

"You have a beautiful heart, Sean."

"Do I?" he asks quietly, still staring at our hands.

"It's resilient and strong. Far more than I can say about my own, which was in such a bitter state when I first met you. I'm amazed at what you've endured. Sean, you give *me* hope that someday I can be fully healed—as strong and resilient as you."

I hear him breathe out a happy sigh. "I'm glad. If any gift I've given you in return for everything you've done for me, I'm glad it's hope."

"Can I tell you something, Sean?"

He looks at me fully.

I turn to him. "It's your decision whether you stay here or not. And you can make that decision whenever you want, whether it's tomorrow, a year from now, or in five and a half minutes. But I want to share everything in my heart with you first. That way, you can make an informed decision. You will know everything."

"O-Okay."

I bring a hand to his cheek, caressing him. "Sean, I feel deep affection for you. Maybe even love. Let me be crystal clear about this: I *want* you to stay with me."

265

His lips part.

"And if you want to stay," I go on, "I will do whatever it takes to keep you safe. And it will be my pleasure to do so. And it's not just about keeping you safe, Sean. I want to keep you smiling, too, because damn, your smile is like the sun breaking over the sky every morning, and this world needs more of it. I want to make you breakfast when you wake up and feed you fudgy cake in my car. I want to take you to every midnight movie and walk home holding your hand. I want to fall asleep every night with you in my arms. I want everything for you, Sean."

I can see the fire in his eyes when he hears my words. I see him living the life I'm picturing for us. The dream. The fantasy made real. The possibilities at his fingertips.

"Coop?"

I'm like the dog he's got by the leash. "Yes, Sean?"

"Before I make my decision … can we stay here for a while longer? Can we just sit right here next to each other and listen to the waves?"

I put my arm around him. "Of course we can." He lays his head on my shoulder as we sit together in the company of mighty, roaring waves and gusting winds. Nothing in the world can touch us in this moment. Sean and I are exactly where we're meant to be—*even if it's just for this one last night on the boardwalk.*

FINALE

SEANY

IT WASN'T AS EASY A DECISION AS I THOUGHT IT'D BE.

I was in a difficult place that night. My heart was in so much pain. I felt heavy and guilty for accepting all the help I'd been given by kindhearted people. I held so many dark thoughts and doubts in my head that I swear they weighed a thousand pounds.

I wonder if anyone will truly understand how I could have possibly considered turning down this little piece of paradise I now call home.

Maybe I've just been conditioned my whole life to not believe in anything that's too good to be true.

"I really hate the fall," moans Mars.

"Why? It's so peaceful!"

"Easy for you to say, *Sean*," she groans as she sits on the front step of the Easy Breezy next to me, staring out at the uncharacteristically empty Sugarberry Beach. "Island's a ghost town on Tuesdays. Weirdest day of the week. You only like it because it's your first fall in Dreamwood."

"It feels like we've got the whole island to ourselves." I smile up at the sunshine, feeling as free as the breeze.

"It won't feel that way on the weekends. Trust me, the summers are bad, but the first several weekends of the fall are worse. Everyone gets horny, weird, and wild chasing some relief from all that workplace stress."

"Hmm. I like it," I decide. "Everything in moderation."

She shakes her head, studying me. "Nothing ever fazes you anymore, huh? Happy-go-lucky? Go with the flow?"

"Easy breezy," I agree, still smiling.

But what I've learned about things that seem too good to be true is that sometimes, there's no harm in trying. How can I go the rest of my life distrusting everything? How can I let my past have such unchecked power over me?

All that pain is like a tyrant standing over me, and it's way past overdue for that fucker to be overthrown.

Assuming it *can* be completely overthrown.

"First weekend will be the *real* test," states Mars, "for whether *Bossy Manager Chase* can handle his new title."

That's Mars's loving new way of addressing Chase, whom Cooper lovingly promoted at the end of the summer to the flashier and more responsibility-bearing role of bar manager, giving Cooper more room to breathe. Mars thinks the title has gone to his head, making him bossy and full of himself. I just see a guy who's finally finding his own inner confidence and trying it out.

I guess I can relate to that sentiment a bit.

Also, I think Chase is doing a *great* job.

"He can handle it," I decide on his behalf. "And if he freaks out a bit, we'll support him, won't we, miss official bar girl Mars?"

She smirks. Chase isn't the only change of staff made over the past month. "At least my mom didn't freak out when I said I didn't want to be under her thumb all the time anymore. Besides, Easy Breezy is more my vibe."

"You *do* realize you'll just be pulled back over to the taqueria whenever the bar's slow, right?"

"We'll see about that. Oh!" She whips out her phone. "Vann just texted. Everyone's meeting up at the arcade. Something about classes on campus being canceled for the day. Should we go and try taking Toby down a peg?"

I grin. "Why not?"

To most Dreamwood residents, Tuesdays are probably boring and uneventful. The waves lazily rush in and the waves lazily pull back. Gulls fly circles over the empty beaches. The Hopewell Fair is shut down, its colorful rides sleeping and silent. The shops are mostly closed, too. Only a few spots are open for the locals.

But to me, even the boring days are treasures.

I'm starting to trust the "too good to be true".

When Mars and I arrive, the arcade feels like it's the liveliest spot on the Texas coast. Toby and Vann face off at the air hockey table with a crowd of familiar faces. Among them is the arcade manager Mr. Buchinski, affectionately known as Mikey B, who cheers on his new favorite gamer Toby. There's also Skipper and his two best friends Reef and Dwayne, who I've gotten to know over the past month. Skip's eighteen now, no longer the baby of his clique, and I hear his brothers Kent and Adrian have been trying to talk him into college once he finishes his senior year, insisting they can help with the tuition.

Among Vann's "arty friends", as Mars so nicely put it, I spot several I regularly worked with, including Lily. The second Lily spots me, she rushes up to me to gush about her latest photoshoot idea. I have to assume at some point since that one awful night when SJ and Lily insinuated I got myself a sugar daddy, Vann had words with them, because the next time I saw them, they were far more respectful. By then, I'd practically forgotten what upset me in the first place. And how can I hold a grudge anyway? From the two of them alone, I've gotten at least a dozen other regular clients all around the campus, and even some local artist alums. I raised my modeling fee per their advice and am looking forward to a busy fall schedule full of gigs.

And if all continues to go well with my GED, maybe by spring I can consider myself a student among them, too.

Fingers crossed.

For the first time in my life, things are truly looking up. I never thought happiness like this could be possible. That I could live and breathe among such a crowd of people and feel like I truly belong. That I wouldn't be living the rest of my days searching over my shoulder for suspicious sounds and dangerous things.

Of course, a part of that "runaway Seany" will always stay inside me. But I've learned to live with him better and share the space of my heart like amicable roommates as best as I can. Some days are a struggle. Most days aren't.

I haven't seen Ice again.

I guess Drake's empty threat worked.

I wonder if Ice ever made it to Houston.

"What're you doing just standing there?" Vann shouts out playfully at me. "Come up to the table and help me kick my boyfriend's ass."

I grin, take hold of the spare air hockey paddle, and get to work on the assignment. Toby, who gets notably cocky when he's in the heat of a competitive game, prepares to take us on, all his friendliness gone as he narrows his eyes and readies the puck.

And an hour later when the whole gang of us flood the Desert Moon Diner, Vann and I are celebrated as the first people to take down Toby at the arcade. Granted, it's not the first time. And we were paired up two against one. But somehow, everyone still considers it a victory as we crowd one table in the middle of the diner (instead of spreading out to two tables like reasonable people) and devour tacos, tortilla chips, and way too much salsa.

Somewhere in the noise of laughter and conversation, I find myself remembering a night I sat by the Gulf with Cooper at my side. I had just told him I made my decision. We sat in silence for what felt like hours, holding each other as the waves crashed and the wind tossed our hair.

I told him: "I want to be your boyfriend."

I felt his body tense up. "What?"

Maybe the wind or the water was too loud. "I want to be your boyfriend," I repeated. "I don't want to be the kid you took off the street. I don't want to be the question mark who runs around your bar. I need to be something real in this place … something I already feel in my heart. I know you feel it in yours."

"Sean …"

"You said you loved me."

He went silent right then. I remember how my heart hammered in my chest. I had so many emotions raging inside me that night.

"I heard you," I told him. "I heard you say it. And I …
I wanted to say it back. But … I was scared. I'm not scared
anymore." I lifted my head off his shoulder and looked at
him. "If I stay here in Dreamwood, then I'm staying here
as your boyfriend. That's my condition, Cooper. My only
condition."

He thought it through for a moment. "And what if we
don't last?"

I didn't blame him for the question. It was an honest
question. A realistic and mature point of view.

I didn't realize how much I would come to appreciate
the honest way he approached such questions. It helped me
gain trust in him. It helped me see he was never motivated
by selfish reasons when it came to what he did for me. He
always had my best interest. He considered every angle. He
was analytical and compassionate.

And so it was with due respect that I answered just as
honestly. "Then at least we tried. And I'd still be grateful
to you for keeping your door open just as you promised."

He weighed that for a moment. Then he gazed upon me
with affection. "You're beautiful, Sean. You know that?"

"Is that a yes?"

Then he kissed me. I closed my eyes and melted into it,
feeling like every bit of pain I had been holding inside my
heavy chest was worth it just to experience the fire we'd

kindled between each other over the summer. Cooper was my boyfriend. I was his boyfriend. We'd start confidently calling ourselves a couple.

But the question remained: would it last?

It was the very next morning—after a long night spent in Cooper's arms, where emotional comforting turned into pent-up frustration in desperate need of release—that I got a very different question answered. I was sent on a quick errand across the street from the bar to the Elysian to pick something up from the handsome manager Armando, when I ran into a familiar face in the lobby.

It was Pearl with a rose-colored rolling suitcase.

Her eyes lit up when she saw me. As if I'd become her actual grandson, she came right up to me and gave me an unexpectedly bone-crushing hug, and said how very happy she was to catch me on her way out. Her husband had gone to pull the car up to the front, so it was only with her that I got to chat a little bit. She said she was headed home a bit earlier than expected on account of something to do with a "particularly needy son-in-law" issue she wouldn't go into much detail about, except that she's always the one to come to her family's aid, even if it's inconvenient or cuts their little vacation short.

"But that's beside the point," she said as she patted me on the shoulder. "You look so happy and healthy, sonny. I didn't mean to startle you yesterday afternoon. You and …

and your Uncle Don seemed to be having a lovely time."

It was right then that I realized I didn't want any more dishonest relationships in my life. I had to come clean. I owed it to the woman who might have unknowingly saved my life.

So I gave her two truths. "My name is Sean."

She smiled warmly at me. "Sean. What a beautiful—"

"And that wasn't my Uncle Don. I … I don't have an Uncle Don. That man was Cooper. He's my boyfriend."

Her smile broke.

Remember that thing about if something's too good to be true? And my insistence on believing in them anyway?

I was ready for this day to be the last day I'd know the old lady. I was ready to be thankful for what she'd done for me—and also bid her farewell when she learned too much.

I was ready for all of that.

Then she said: "Well, my sweet boy, if you thought I didn't already know that, you're just plain silly."

It was my turn to lift my eyebrows in surprise.

She spread her hands. "Have you forgotten where we are? The gayest place on the Texas coast! My husband and I *adore* Dreamwood Isle. We come here once a month."

I had been rendered officially speechless.

I don't know what I expected.

"My sweet grandson works here at the Elysian and gets us discounted rooms. Oh, did I not mention that part? My

grandson I told you about ... you *so* remind me of him."
She beamed as she said that last part, then put a hand on
my arm. "Thank you for telling me the truth, sonny, Sean. I
can't even express in words without crying like a baby how
happy I am that you found a home here."

I apparently couldn't express my own emotions in
words either, so I just returned her hug with a happy one of
my own.

It wasn't the last time we saw each other.

Every time she and her husband are in town, I make
sure to drop by the Elysian, and I can always find her by
the pool reading a book, just like she promised.

I call her Grandma Pearl now.

She welcomes it.

After all the college kids take off back to campus, the
day stretches on with us locals strolling around town. We
hang out at the park while Skipper and his friends show off
their skateboard moves on the old basketball court. Then
we lounge on the beach in the late afternoon, shirts off,
baking in the sun while waiting for evening to roll around.
Toby and Vann play with each other in the water. Skipper
and his friends eventually take off back to his house,
leaving me and Mars the whole blanket to spread out on.

Mars peers over at me. "So have you heard from him
yet?"

I check my phone, then shake my head. "*Nada.*"

"Really? It's been all day."

"I know."

"Are things … alright with you guys?"

"Yeah." I put my hands behind my head with a relaxed sigh. "No news isn't bad news."

She's not convinced. "It isn't good news either."

"Don't worry, Mars. Everything will be fine." Toby's laugher rings out after wrestling Vann into the water. The two grapple playfully, trying to overpower each other. I smile and close my eyes, drinking in the last of the day's generous sunshine.

Chase opens the bar at five, looking smart in his dress shirt and bowtie—which are in no way a required uniform, but he insists on dressing up for his new role, wanting to "feel the part". After an hour, a surprising amount of locals drop in for beer, laughter, and good conversation, keeping the Easy Breezy full of love and warmth. The crowd ebbs around seven, and soon, the bar is calm and quiet. Toby and Vann finally head home. Mars takes off soon after. Chase mans the front of the bar with a proud smile, now and then fidgeting too much and deciding to clean tables that have already been cleaned, too restless to stand still.

It's while washing dishes in the kitchen that I hear the back door open. I lift my head from a sink full of suds to find Cooper having come in. His white dress shirt is rolled up at the sleeves and his tie is slightly askew, which isn't how I sent him off this morning from the house.

When he sees me, he comes to a stop as the heavy door shuts behind him. I see the stress in his eyes. I feel a world of questions swelling between us in the silence, which is only filled by the hum of kitchen appliances and the faucet still running at the sink.

I shut off the faucet without looking and grab hold of a towel. "Cooper."

"Sean," he greets me back with half a sigh.

"Haven't heard from you all day." I set the towel down and take a step forward. "I thought the worst."

"I figured. I'm ... sorry."

Staring into each other's eyes right now, it's not easy to pinpoint exactly what I'm feeling. I imagine he feels the same, especially after spending the whole day apart. Just a month ago, we decided to be boyfriends. We committed to seeing this through. We became determined to finding out whether what we have will last.

He comes to the side of the sink. "Been a long day."

"I can imagine." I lift my eyebrows expectantly. "Are you okay?"

He peers into my eyes. A smile slowly spreads over his face. "Now that I'm with you, I'm perfect."

I smile back. "Are you going to tell me how it went?"

"Yes. But first ..." He produces a white box, which I didn't notice he had hidden behind his back. "For us."

I blink. "Our favorite cake from Thalassa?"

"I know you're not one for anniversaries, and I've been gone all day on the mainland, but ..." He smiles. "I thought we should maybe celebrate our one-month."

"Our one-month?"

"Our *real* one-month ... as an official couple." He leans into me. "Hey, thinking back to how we enjoyed this cake last time, do you want to—"

"—sit in your car in the parking lot and feed each other bites? *Yes*," I finish for him. "A thousand times *yes*."

With that, the pair of us make a sneaky retreat through the back door before anyone even knows Cooper's here. In another minute, we're cuddled up in his car sharing bites of decadent triple chocolate melting cake from Thalassa with cheap plastic forks. I take this as Adrian's way of cheering us on for finding each other and making it this far.

And as if tonight couldn't become more magical: "The investor said yes," Cooper tells me.

I gasp. "Are you serious??"

"Yep. He's going to help out with expanding the bar."

"That's amazing, Coop! I'm so happy for you!"

"For me? Baby, it's for *us*."

I feed him another forkful. "Yeah, but the Easy Breezy is *your* baby—and your family's pride. Imagine how happy your mom and dad are gonna be when you tell them!"

"Oh, they already know." Coop chuckles as he returns

the favor by feeding me a bite. "I called them in the car on the way back. My dad is ecstatic. My mom was in tears. I think even my grandma heard and was so happy for me. It's gonna be a lot of hard work, it'll take lots of planning, and it won't happen overnight, but my new investor knows this town's popularity. He sees where the Easy Breezy can go with some time and lovin'." He takes hold of my hand. "Sean ... do you realize you were my inspiration today?"

"Me?"

"You gave me renewed hope. You gave me the vision. The dream. And to know that after a hard day like today, I could come back home to your sweet face?" His eyes turn soft as he rubs my hand. "None of this means anything without you in my life, Sean."

I'm nearly in tears when he's finished. "Coop ..."

He lifts another bite with the fork. "Happy anniversary. Here's to many more months."

I take my own fork and cut a bite, then clink it against his in a cheer. "To many more."

We smile as we finish the rest of the cake in the peace and quiet of his car, which sits under a blanket of twinkling stars. He tells me more about how the interview went. How the building was too cold, but he didn't complain. How he was so nervous this morning and so deliriously happy on his way home. His muscles ache. He's exhausted from the long day. It sounds like he could use a nice rubbing down, a hot shower, and some tender love and care.

The cake has long since been finished, the box closed and sitting on the dash. We clasp each other's hands over the center console. "Today has been amazing," I tell him. "This magical night, even more amazing. I think Tuesday just became my new favorite day of the week."

"Really? I thought that was Sunday?"

"Any day of the week I'm here is a good day." I lean over the console, putting my face in front of his. "Y'know what would make our life even more perfect?"

His eyes are lost in mine. "What's that?"

"Two dogs. One named King. The other, Rook."

That wasn't what he was expecting. "Really?"

"And you gotta bake chocolate chip cookies. Cookies with a magic ingredient—with your love all in them. Then this place will be the exact paradise I dreamed of."

He laughs. "If that's what makes you happy. Anything for my Seany baby."

"You're the best, Coopy." I lean in for a kiss. Every time our lips unite, I know I'm home.

The end.

OTHER WORKS BY DARYL BANNER

Spruce Texas Romances (M/M)

Football Sundae ·

Born Again Sinner ·

Heteroflexible ·

Wrangled ·

Rebel At Spruce High ·

Summer Sweat ·

Hopeful Romantic ·

(more to come...)

Texas Beach Town Romances (M/M)

In Too Deep ·

Crusher ·

Far From Paradise ·

(more to come ...)

Stand-alone Romances & Novels (M/M)

Getting Lucky ·

Bromosexual ·

Hard For My Boss ·

Raising Hell ·

When I See You Again ·

Lover's Flood ·

Jerk ·

Boys & Toys (M/M)

Caysen's Catch / Wade's Workout / Dean's Dare / Garret's Game ·

Season 2: Connor / Brett / Dante / Zak ·

Holiday-Centric Romances (M/M)

My Bad Ex-Boyfriend (Valentine's) ·
Making The Naughty List (Christmas) ·
My Ghost Roommate Who Helps Me Get The Guy (Halloween) ·
My Pumpkin Prince And The Ghost Between Us (Halloween) ·

The Brazen Boys (M/M)

Dorm Game ·
On The Edge ·
Owned By The Freshman ·
Dog Tags / Commando ·
All Yours Tonight ·
Straight Up ·
Houseboy Rules ·
Slippery When Wet ·

A College Obsession Romance (M/F)

Read My Lips ·
Beneath The Skin ·
With These Hands ·
Through Their Eyes: Five Years Later ·

The Beautiful Dead Saga (Post-Apocalyptic Fantasy)

The Beautiful Dead / Dead Of Winter / Almost Alive ·
The Whispers / Winter's Doom / Deathless ·

The OUTLIER Series (Epic Dystopian)

Rebellion / Legacy / Reign Of Madness ·
Beyond Oblivion / Weapons Of Atlas / Gifts Of The Goddess ·
The Slum Queen / The Twice King / Queen Of Wrath ·

Printed in Great Britain
by Amazon

20508035R00165